Nurse Alissa vs.

the Zombies IV:

Hunters

Scott M. Baker

Nurse Alissa vs. the Zombies IV: Hunters

Also by Scott M. Baker

Novels
Nurse Alissa vs. the Zombies
Nurse Alissa vs. the Zombies: Escape
Nurse Alissa vs. the Zombies III: Firestorm
Shattered World I: Paris
Shattered World II: Russia
Shattered World III: China
Shattered World IV: Japan
The Vampire Hunters
Vampyrnomicon
Dominion
Rotter World
Rotter Nation
Rotter Apocalypse
Yeitso

Novellas
Nazi Ghouls From Space
Twilight of the Living Dead
This Is Why We Can't Have Nice Things During the Zombie Apocalypse

Anthologies
Cruise of the Living Dead and other Stories
Incident on Ironstone Lane and Other Horror Stories

A Schattenseite Book

Nurse Alissa vs. the Zombies IV: Hunters
by Scott M. Baker.
Copyright © 2020. All Rights Reserved.
Print Edition
ISBN-13: 978-1-7351312-4-5

Cover Art © Christian Bentulan

To my niece Kiera and my nephew Stevie.

I love you guys like you were my own children.

Chapter One

"CAN WE TAKE a break?" Sheri leaned against a tree. She slipped off the Red Sox baseball cap and ran her palm across her forehead, wiping away the sweat. "We've been walking for hours."

"Nut up," replied David. "It's only been ninety minutes since our last break."

"That's still a long time."

Tina grunted in frustration. "Why did we have to bring the prom queen along?"

"Because nobody gets left behind." Brad snapped, quickly ending the argument. The three had been at each other's throats for weeks. If they kept bickering, Brad might throw himself into a pack of deaders so he wouldn't have to listen to them. It would be quicker and less painful.

"Take five."

David and Tina groaned, quieting down when John flashed them an angry glare. They wandered off to get away from the group for a few minutes. Sheri mouthed "Thank you." She slid down the tree into a crouch, opened a bottle of water, and took a long drink. Brad strolled over to a fallen log, sat down, and sighed. He didn't know how much more of this he could take.

The group had been together since the outbreak began. They were students at Endicott College north of Salem, Massachusetts. Everyone else on campus had been locals and left to be with their loved ones. Brad and several students from out of state assumed it would all be over soon so they opted to shelter in place. How long could the civil unrest last? Between the food in their dorms and what they had scavenged from the cafeteria, they had enough supplies to last for weeks. It would not be enough. As the realization dawned on them they were not dealing with rioters but the living dead, and that none of them would be going home in the near future, the group moved to the second floor of their dorm, filled the stairwells with furniture to prevent the deaders from reaching them, and hunkered down to wait it out.

At that time, there were twenty-nine of them.

They had holed up for two weeks before the deaders occupying the campus stumbled across them by accident. The next five weeks devolved into a siege that ended when a freshman named Randy cracked under the pressure and cleared out a stairwell trying to escape, inadvertently letting the deaders in. The dorm became a slaughterhouse. Only eleven students escaped and headed north.

For some reason, the survivors had turned to Brad for leadership, probably because he was the only senior classman among them. He led the survivors toward what hopefully would be the relative safety of Canada which, at the time, seemed the best option. Three and a half years of college had not prepared him for what they faced out here, and experience came at a high cost. By the time he had figured out how to avoid a deader horde and survive an attack, too many of his group had become casualties. Of those who set out from Endicott, four had been killed by deaders, one died from the elements, and one had taken her own life to spare herself from this nightmare. Their deaths had taught Brad to avoid main roads and travel through the woods. The going had been slow, but it kept them safe. It also kept them cold, tired, and hungry.

John came over and sat beside Brad, taking Brad's hand in his own and squeezing gently. "You okay?"

"Yes," Brad lied. Then he thought better of it. "Not really. I don't know how much longer I can go on."

John chuckled.

"What's so funny?"

"You've said that every week for the past two months, then you pick yourself up and keep going. None of us would have made it this far without you."

"Tell that to Jesse, Sandy, Kevin, and the others."

"They lasted as long as they did because of you. It's not your fault they're dead. This brave, new, fucked up world killed them."

"That's easy for you—"

John placed two fingers on Brad's lips. "You've done a great job. None of us would be following you if we didn't trust you."

Brad winked. "You'd still be here, I hope."

"I would, but I'm biased." John leaned in and kissed Brad. "Time to move out."

They joined Sheri.

"Break time's over," said Brad.

Sheri groaned. She placed the Red Sox cap back on her head, pulling her ponytail through the opening over the back straps.

"Where's Tina and David?" asked John.

Sheri shrugged as she stood, then pointed to an area where the woods were less dense. "They headed in that direction. I assumed they were looking for a place to do it."

"Shit," mumbled Brad.

John tried to lighten the mood. "At least they've gotten down the repopulate the world part."

Tina emerged from the woods and whistled. Once she caught their attention, she motioned for them to follow, which they did. When they caught up with her, Brad asked, "Is there a problem?"

"Everything's fine."

"Where's David?"

"There." Tina pointed in front of them.

A field one hundred acres square stretched before them, two-thirds of it having been enclosed by a wooden fence. A stable sat inside the fence on the opposite side of the enclosure and, just beyond it, a farmhouse. A dozen horses grazed outside the stable, keeping wary eyes on the seven predators reaching across the fence, their hands futilely clutching for the food.

"What's going on?" asked John.

"As far as I can tell," answered David, "those deaders stumbled across the corral and tried to feed off the horses. The farmer went to stop them and was turned."

"Why do you think that?"

"The horses are in great shape. They're well fed and hydrated, which means someone has been taking care of them until recently." David gestured toward a freshly reanimated deader in the center of the pack. "More than likely him."

"So?" Sheri asked in a snarky tone. "How does this involve us?"

"Those horses mean we don't have to walk anymore."

"Oh?" Sheri suddenly showed interest.

Brad faced her and grinned. "Now we ride in style."

"Once we get rid of those things," said David, referring to the deaders.

"Let's do this." John led the way to the fence.

Tina whistled to catch the attention of the living dead. They turned as one toward the new source of food. Six of them moaned and staggered in their direction. The farmer, only recently having been turned, snarled and rushed them, closing the distance rapidly.

"I got this," said Brad as he positioned himself in front of Tina. He brandished the baseball bat he carried. Tina stayed ten feet to his rear, ready to help if necessary.

Brad waited until the deader had come closer and timed his strike carefully. Once within range, he swung the bat, his upper body turning to add additional energy. It connected with the

4

farmer's head, caving in the left side of its skull. The farmer spun to the right and stumbled but did not go down. As it turned to face its prey, Brad swung the bat again, this time connecting with the deader's neck. It collapsed into the grass and spasmed. Tina stepped up, positioned the three-foot-long crowbar above its head, and plunged the straight claw through its left eye, churning the metal around to scramble its brain. The deader's body went limp.

Sheri crossed herself. "Peace be with you. Go with God."

The rest confronted the other deaders, spreading out in a line abreast to present scattered targets. Weeks of experience came in handy. Brad struck down two more with his bat. Tina drove the crowbar through the eye of a third, again churning it around until the deader collapsed. John lifted his axe and brought it down through the head of the fourth, cleaving it open until the blade reached its jaw. David used his machete to decapitate the fifth. Sheri moved in against the last deader, a teenage woman in a soiled high school t-shirt. Clutching its collar in her gloved hand, she drove her bowie knife up and into the left side of its neck, puncturing the brain stem, then twisted. The deader slid off the blade into the grass. As the others approached the corral, Sheri stayed behind to give the same last rites to each corpse as she had done with the farmer.

The horses eyed the newcomers cautiously. One of them, a tan American Trotter, made its way over to the fence, sensing these people posed no threat. Tina held out her hand. The horse drew closer, sniffing her palm. Tina placed her hand on the side of its nose and gently rubbed.

"You're a friendly girl."

The horse playfully nibbled at her hand.

Thirty minutes later, the group had settled in the farmer's house, after searching it for deaders or survivors, finding neither. John returned from checking the stable.

"There are four more horses inside. They're a bit skittish but healthy."

"What about saddles?" asked David.

"There's one for each horse, so we won't have to ride bareback."

"God be praised," Sheri replied.

"Then it's settled," said Brad. "We'll stay here for the night. Tomorrow we'll take five of the horses and head out."

"What about the others?" asked Tina.

"We'll give them all the hay we can find and leave the corral gate open. That way they'll have a fighting chance."

"Thank you."

David came down from upstairs. "There are two bedrooms. One has a king size bed, the other a double."

"Excellent. The girls can share the bigger bed and you can take the double. John and I will take the sofa and recliner."

"I hope this place has hot water," said Sheri. "I could use a nice shower."

"We all could," added Tina.

Brad turned to John, "Check out the kitchen for food. Hopefully, there's something for a good meal. I'll make sure the doors are secured."

Everyone set off about their business, looking forward to the first comfortable night since leaving Endicott.

Chapter Two

MIRIAM HELD BRIAN'S hand, raising his arm off the bed. Alissa placed onto the mattress a makeshift splint she had constructed out of a piece of cardboard cut and folded into a three-sided, L-shaped brace lined with towels. Once in place, Miriam lowered his arm. The limb rested snugly inside. Alissa packed the rest of the splint with towels and secured it to Brian's arm with a generous amount of roller gauze and adhesive tape. When finished, she put the remaining medical supplies back into the first aid kit.

"Thanks for helping," said Alissa.

"No problem." Miriam used a facecloth to wipe the boy's forehead. "What's next?"

"We let him sleep."

"Do you want me to stay?"

"I'll check in on him later." Alissa closed the kit's lid. "Besides, I'm sure Diana will want to be with him."

The two women exited Nathan's bedroom, which had been turned into Brian's recovery room. Diana jumped up from the sofa and met them at the bottom of the stairs.

"How's Brian?"

"He's fine." Alissa placed a comforting hand on Diana's. "He's asleep right now. I gave him some extra morphine for the pain."

"Is it that bad?"

"He'll be in pain for a while. The break was severe, but Rebecca did a good job setting it. I used Crazy Glue on the breaks, sewed up the wound, and set it in a splint."

"Will he be…?" Diana could not bring herself to complete the sentence.

"Crippled? No. But he may have limited mobility in it."

Diana closed her eyes. "Thank God."

Connie joined them. "Can I see my brother?"

"Of course. He'll want you there when he wakes up." Alissa crouched. "He's going to need a lot of help the next few weeks until I can take off the splint. Can I count on you?"

"Me?" Connie beamed. "Of course."

"Good. Why don't you go sit with him?"

"Okay." Connie ran upstairs.

Diana followed, pausing to hug Alissa. "Thank you."

"You're welcome."

Alissa headed into the kitchen to pour herself and Miriam a cup of coffee, sweetened with a shot of rum. Diana and her kids, as well as Rebecca, were the newcomers to the group, having been saved during a gunfight with a gang of assholes that had ambushed her people in North Conway, hoping to take over her cabin. Alissa's people had lucked out three times yesterday: defeating the gang with no losses among themselves, saving those imprisoned, and surviving the forest fire that had raged around them.

Bringing the two cups of coffee back into the dining room, Alissa placed one in front of Miriam and sat opposite her friend, taking a long swig from her mug.

"That's good."

Miriam tasted her coffee. "You could have added a little more rum."

Steve, who sat at the end of the table, grinned. "You could have brought me a cup of coffee."

"You're not crippled," Miriam replied.

Steve exaggeratedly gestured to his leg wounded a few weeks ago when he accidentally dropped an axe on it.

Too tired to stop their bickering, Alissa avoided it by asking

Stephen, "Where's Rebecca?"

"She's taking a nap in the kids' room."

"Did you find out anything about them?"

"Diana and her family had sheltered in place at their home but had to abandon it when deaders overran the neighborhood. They escaped in the family Hummer and did well for themselves until they were captured by that gang about a month ago. Diana and her husband would go into stores and search for supplies, hunting out any deaders. Dickson's gang used her every night for sex."

"Were the kids…?"

"No one sexually or physically abused them. They were ransom to make sure Diana and her husband obeyed. The boy got his arm broke in a confrontation with the deaders."

"What about Diana's husband?"

"The gang leader shot him a week ago when he mouthed off to him. From what her and Rebecca told me, that guy was a real asshole."

"That's for sure." Alissa flashed back to the fight in the hotel office when Dickson had ordered Nathan executed and shot his own girlfriend in the ensuing battle. "What about Rebecca?"

"Pretty much the same story. Her and her boyfriend survived on their own until they ran into the gang about a week ago. Only in Rebecca's case, her boyfriend allowed her to be passed around the gang like a joint at a frat party so he could be part of the crew."

"What happened to him?"

"She knocked him out during the fight with the deaders and escaped with Diana's family. He died in the propane explosion outside of Lowe's."

"She never mentioned him to us."

Steve shrugged. "I guess by that time he was dead to her."

Alissa could not begin to imagine what Diana and Rebecca, as well as the kids, had gone through. Their experiences made her appreciate how well off the rest of them were.

"It's horrible," said Miriam.

Alissa agreed. "So many who go on the run wind up either eaten or as sex toys for a gang."

"It's the new norm," added Steve.

"That sucks," chimed in Miriam, a hint of depression in her tone. "Is this what society has become?"

"It'll get better," said Alissa with a sense of false hope. "It has to or people will give up and die. We can't let that happen."

An awkward silence followed.

Steve broke the mood. "Are they going to stay with us?"

"For now. Which reminds me," began Alissa, brokering a touchy subject. "Would you mind if the kids bunked with you?"

"Of course not," said Miriam.

"Though I'm sure the princess will bitch about it," added Steve.

"She'll get over it." Miriam's mom voice kicked in.

"Thanks. I wanted to put Diana and the kids in Little Steve's room and Rebecca in Kiera's."

"Where will Nathan sleep?" Miriam's question had a sultry tone to it.

"Shit. I forgot about him."

Steve laughed. "I promise not to tell him."

Miriam grinned. "He could sleep with you."

Alissa quickly changed topics. "Where are they?"

"They're outside checking on the vehicles."

"Let me guess. Kiera is with them."

Steve nodded. Miriam rolled her eyes.

Alissa stood and headed for the door. "I'll go save them."

Chapter Three

"**H**OW IS IT?" asked Kiera as they stared at the caved in passenger door of the Ram.

"It drives fine," answered Chris. "You can't open and close the side doors. Plus, the windows are busted out and I don't know how to replace them. Whoever sits there would be exposed to deaders."

"That's okay," said Nathan. "Next time we're in town we'll ditch the Ram for a pick-up."

"What a shame. I liked the idea of going into battle with this."

Nathan frowned. "Too much of a gas guzzler."

That's the difference between you and me, thought Chris. *You're the cautious type. I go for what I want.*

Except Alissa.

Chris tried to push that thought out of his head. Easier said than done. He had the hots for Alissa from the first day he had met her, even when she had a shotgun pointed at him ready to shoot. Of course, that could be his way of thinking. He liked strong women. The only reason he had not made his desires clear was because of the situation with Nathan. He knew Nathan wanted to be with her. Yet it didn't seem like Alissa and Nathan were an item. Sure, the two of them were close but, as far as he could tell, they weren't involved. Chris also got the vibe that Alissa really liked him. Well, maybe not *really* liked him. She didn't detest him, which counted for something. Normally he would have asked her out by now and being afraid to make a move irked him. But the last thing the group needed during the apocalypse was a love triangle.

The front door to the cabin closed and Alissa came down the steps. Chris checked her out. She had a nice figure and, truth be told, he had imagined her naked several times. It went beyond beauty. Alissa was smart, tough, independent, and could hold her own in combat better than most guys he knew. That combination attracted him more than anything.

"Kiera," Alissa said as she approached, smiling. "Are you bothering Chris and Nathan?"

"I'm trying," she responded flirtatiously. "They're more interested in the Ram."

"Is there anything wrong with it?"

"It's mobile," answered Chris. "The propane tank did some major damage to the door."

"Whose fault is that?" asked Nathan.

Before Chris could respond, Alissa came to his defense.

"Granted, shooting the propane tanks was a bit extreme, but it saved us from a horde of deaders." Alissa walked around the Ram, examining its condition. "Only be more careful next time. We only have so many cars."

Chris took being chastised in good nature. "I figure we can get another in better condition next time we go off compound."

"That will be tomorrow or the day after."

"Why so soon?" asked Chris.

"I want to set up a roadblock across the driveway as soon as possible. We're lucky Nora came by herself to lure us into town. If they had tried an armed assault, we probably would have been overrun."

"How would a roadblock stop them?" asked Nathan.

"It wouldn't, but it'd slow them down enough to give us time to prepare. I also want it to look like it belongs here."

"You mean like a fallen tree?" asked Kiera.

Chris shook his head. "We could chop down a tree easy enough, but it would be impossible to move. We'd have to leave the cars outside the compound."

"If you don't want to draw attention to us," began Nathan, "I recommend a chain link fence with a gate or a double- or single-arm swing gate. The first would give us more protection but the latter would be easier to install."

"I prefer the chain link fence. It offers more protection. Can we extend the fence around the cabin?"

Chris and Nathan stared at each other and then back to Alissa. Chris answered for both. "We could, but there's a lot of work involved—"

Alissa interrupted. "Steve is back on his feet and we now have Rebecca and Diana."

"—and it would require either constantly going back to the store to pick up enough fence or stealing a flatbed truck, both of which will attract a lot of attention."

"Plus," added Nathan, "while a chain link fence in the middle of the woods will stop the deaders, it'll look suspicious to any humans and will draw attention to us."

Kiera cleared her throat to get their attention. "What about stringing two or three more strands of barbed wire around the compound. It'll have the same effect as a chain link fence and not stand out as much."

Chris patted Kiera on the shoulder, eliciting a warm smile. "Her idea is best."

"Do you have enough barbed wire to do it?"

"If not, we can pick some up when we get the materials to build the gate."

Alissa nodded her approval. "It's settled. We'll set up a chain link fence in the driveway and increase the barbed wire around the compound. Do you two know what we need to get it all done?"

Chris and Nathan stared at each other again. Both responded with a yes that didn't sound is if they were certain.

"Since Lowe's burned down, find another place on the map. We'll head out in two days. That'll give us a chance to relax. I want to stay close to Brian in case anything goes wrong with his recovery." Alissa paused. "Which brings up another matter."

Nathan rolled his eyes. "Oh boy."

Kiera snickered.

"What?" Alissa glared at the three of them.

"Whenever anybody uses the phrase 'another matter,' it can't be good," said Chris.

"You sounded like my mother," added Kiera.

Chris chuckled.

"What I wanted to talk to you about are the new living arrangements. Diana and Rebecca will be staying with us for a while. I wanted to put Diana and the kids in your room."

"Where will I sleep?" Kiera asked.

Alissa raised an eyebrow.

"No." Kiera shook her head. "There's no fucking way I'm sleeping in the same room with my parents. Have you ever heard my father snore?"

Chris motioned for her to tone down the language.

Nathan was sterner. "Kiera, we all have to make sacrifices."

"I'm glad to hear you say that." Alissa forced a smile. "I'm giving your room to Rebecca."

"What?"

"We all have to make sacrifices," mimicked Kiera.

Nathan glanced over at Kiera and grinned. "I guess I could sleep on the couch for a while."

"There's enough room in Alissa's bed," said Kiera, only half joking.

Both Nathan and Alissa flashed her a dirty look.

Chris offered a suggestion that got Kiera off the hook and prevented Alissa from agreeing to that horrible idea. "Nathan could stay with me and Shithead. We have plenty of room."

"That's sounds good," Nathan agreed.

Alissa shook her head in frustration. "Then we'd have to call your cabin Testosterone Tower."

Chris grunted.

"We can discuss this later." Alissa headed back to the cabin. "I'm going inside to have lunch and a drink."

"Can you make us a sandwich?" joked Chris.

The finger Alissa raised over her shoulder as she walked away told Chris he would have to make his own lunch.

Chapter Four

ALPHA LED THE pack of deaders along the road, surrounded by his five Betas for protection. They did not stagger aimlessly like the less advanced of their kind but moved steadily with a fierce determination, like every carnivore that sought out prey. Three members scouted twenty-five yards ahead for food and potential danger.

Both were scarce around here. They last fed on that stray human whom they cornered in the gully several days ago. He had satiated their appetite for a while. The insatiable hunger had returned shorty after, that inner force that drove them to constantly wander and hunt.

After feasting on their last human, Alpha had led the pack along the path the human had traveled, hoping to find more food. Instead, they came upon a road and followed it through a landscape of charred trees and grass. None of them recognized that they passed through a burnt-out wasteland devoid of life. They followed the road because experience had taught them the best sources of food followed these paths. The living things that occupied the woods, the things its brain recalled as animals, provided nourishment. They were not as filling or as tasty as humans. For some reason unbeknownst to Alpha, the flesh of humans quelled their appetite more fully than any other creature and provided more sustenance, maintaining their mobility and keeping their minds sharp. That was why Alpha always fed first. The pack could only be maintained if its leader thrived.

Others of their kind had fallen in with them, swelling their numbers and lessening the amount of food each pack member could have. Some adapted, learning from the others how to hunt and scavenge. They proved vital, increasing its numbers and, in turn, its chances of cornering prey. Those that did not adapt straggled along behind, occasionally becoming a feast when the hunger became too great. They had learned long ago that the flesh of their own kind offered the nourishment necessary to keep going, although it did nothing to quell the all-powerful hunger.

The charred forest turned into the burnt wasteland of a town destroyed by fire. None of the pack noticed the change in their surroundings. Nor did they notice the road sign at the entrance of the town, its paint partially seared off by the heat, that welcomed them to North Conway.

The pack spread out and strode through the carnage. Occasionally, they stumbled across a blackened body. One of the pack members would wander over and sniff, determining it belonged to their kind, yet for some reason was not edible. The fifth deader that checked out a carcass dropped to its knees and tore off a chunk of flesh, expecting a moist and tender meal. Instead, the tissue crumbled. Despite this, it shoved the burnt flesh into its mouth, savoring the morsel. Only there was nothing to savor. The meat broke apart in its mouth like ash. The deader gagged and spit out the remains, snarled in frustration, and climbed to its feet.

A commotion erupted to the far right. Some of the deaders on the fringe of the pack had stumbled across two corpses belonging to humans, neither of which had been burned. Both were several days old, and the one that had been torn apart during its death had decayed rapidly and become infested with insects. It didn't matter to the deaders. Scores of those not belonging to the pack descended on the bodies, tearing off chunks of flesh and tissue or ripping out organs, which they fought over. Those lucky enough to grab food shoved the meat into their mouths and ate frantically, a deader feeding frenzy. Those who did not get their fill dropped to their knees and gnawed on the remains, chewing the bones clean.

One of the Betas, dressed in the blood-stained camouflage uniform of a National Guard officer, its arms and torso ravaged in an earlier attack, became angry that the deaders forgot protocol and fed before Alpha. It howled in protest until Alpha stopped it. The deaders feeding first did not belong to the pack and, as such, did not know better. If Alpha could have experienced emotion, it would have been pity. These were the weak links, the unevolved, the least useful and adapted of their breed. They would die out soon from lack of food and an inability to hunt or would become food for the pack. However, Alpha could not relate this to his Beta. It merely groaned, ordering his subordinate to stop, a command readily obeyed.

Alpha led the pack deeper into the scorched town. It expressed no concern over the lack of prey. Experience had taught Alpha to stay alert and keep moving. Food would eventually come to them.

Chapter Five

"WE'RE ON A lucky streak," said John.

"I'm not complaining," Brad responded as he lay spread out in a hammock. "I've got my fingers crossed it'll continue."

The group had lucked out big time. Yesterday they had found the horses and spent the night at the farmhouse recharging with a long, restful sleep in real beds in the safety of an isolated home. All of them had overslept, though God knew they needed to. Brad had wanted to spend another night there. The others out voted him, wanting to continue while things were going well. Although they started late, the group had traversed farther on horseback than they did on foot and were far less exhausted than usual. On top of that, an hour ago they stumbled across this camp site.

Not just any camp site. This one had been set up by experienced outdoors people. It sat adjacent to a fresh-water river with enough space between it and the woods that nothing, living or living dead, could sneak up on them. The camp had three large, heavy-duty tents, a hammock that Brad called dibs on, and a cooler of beer, the ice long since melted. Not that it mattered. It was the first beer any of them had drank since the dead came back to life. Brad wondered what had happened to its occupants. There were no signs of a deader attack, no indications that the owners left in a hurry, or even that anyone other than themselves had been here since being abandoned. Brad refused to look a gift horse in the mouth, pun intended.

David crouched by the river, his hand in the water and enjoying the feel as it flowed by. John and Tina sat in folding chairs on either end of the hammock, drinking warm beer. Sheri strolled around, rubbing her butt.

"What's wrong?" asked Brad.

Sheri squeezed her cheeks. "My ass hurts from all the riding."

"I know how that feels," John whispered.

Tina smirked. Brad burst out laughing.

"What's so funny?" asked Sheri, oblivious to the double entendre.

John steered the conversation in another direction. "At least we found a nice place for the horses for tonight. I worried we'd have to bunker down in another service station."

Sheri made the sign of the cross. "God has been good to us."

"He has," agreed Tina.

David returned from the river. "This place is beautiful. Too bad we can't stay here."

"I hear you," John responded. "Sooner or later either the deaders would find us or we'd run out of supplies."

David sighed.

"Which brings up something I wanted to discuss with all of you." Brad positioned himself so he sat in the hammock. "I think we should abandon going to Canada and head for Nova Scotia instead."

"That'll make the trip even longer," said Sheri.

"We have the horses now, so it won't be that bad. Plus, it'll be safer."

"How so?" asked Tina.

"We're going to have to cross three major highways, all of which I'm sure are overrun by deaders, plus pass through the populated areas around Montreal before we reach safety. If we head northeast, once we cross I-93 it's clear sailing through small towns and forests. If we're lucky, we might even find a good place to shelter in sooner. What do you think?"

"I'm with you," said John.

"I trust in the Lord," added Sheri.

Tina nodded. "I'm in."

Only David seemed reticent.

"You don't agree?"

"It sounds good, I guess."

"What's wrong?" asked John.

David shrugged. "I have a bad feeling."

"About heading for Nova Scotia?"

"No. What you said makes sense. I...." He paused.

"What is it?" asked Brad.

David searched for the right words. "We've been fortunate so far. Too fortunate. My gut tells me there's trouble ahead."

"If we go to Nova Scotia?"

"In general. It's like waiting for the other shoe to drop."

"Trust in the Lord."

David seemed about to snap at Sheri, so Brad jumped in. "I understand where you're coming from."

"I'm being paranoid," said David.

"You're not."

"I am."

Brad slid off the hammock. "Deaders have taken over the planet. As far as we know, we're the last people alive. My reasoning is we stand a better chance if we take the path of least resistance."

"Ah," said John, trying to lighten the mood. "The survival instincts of a physics major."

The others laughed, even Brad. "Would you feel better if we continued north?"

David shook his head. "I'm not going to feel better until we find a place where we don't have to worry about deaders."

"Amen."

"Then it's settled? Tomorrow we head northeast."

Everyone agreed.

"To be on the safe side, we'll post a guard all night. John will take sundown to midnight. I'll take from midnight until dawn."

Chapter Six

ALISSA, NATHAN, AND Kiera gathered around the Land Rover as Chris spread out the map on its hood. Shithead stood on the front porch, barking at Archer who curled up on the inside sill, showing a lot of bravery so long as a glass pane separated him from the cat. Chris whistled to his dog, who ignored him.

"Shithead, get over here."

The dog took a step back, barked three more times at his nemesis, then raced over to rejoin his master. Chris bent and scratched his pet behind the ears.

"Where are we heading this time?" asked Alissa.

Chris straightened up and pointed at a location on the map north of their position. "Gorham, a few miles south of Berlin."

"Berlin?" Nathan glanced between the two adults. "That's where the federal prison is located."

"Why Gorham?" asked Alissa. "Isn't there a Lowe's or Home Depot that's closer?"

"Yeah," chided Nathan. "Why go so far when you could blow up something local?"

Chris ignored his friend. "Everyone flocked to those places and now they're swarming with deaders. Kiera checked the Internet last night—"

"Wait," interrupted Alissa. "The Internet is still working?"

"Only parts of it," answered Kiera. "All social media and news sites are either down or haven't been updated since shortly after the outbreak. Search engines are offline. I happened to stumble across a few Chamber of Commerce websites for the local region. I bookmarked and saved screen-shots of the sites onto the PC."

"Getting back to the main topic." Chris did little to hide his irritation. "Kiera found a private hardware store in Gorham that specializes in supplies for livestock."

"Then they should have all the barbed wire we need for the perimeter defense," said Nathan.

"Exactly." Chris grinned. "Small town, small store, and a good chance there are only a few deaders around to take care of. I thought it was our best bet."

"Agreed," said Alissa. "Good job."

Nathan seemed unconvinced. "Do you think we have enough people to handle what we might run into?"

"I've taken care of that."

As if on cue, Miriam and Rebecca exited the cabin. Miriam carried her Mossberg and Rebecca a .308 R1A1 FN FAL battle rifle.

Kiera sighed. "Mom, come on."

"Alissa asked me to go along to provide back up. I won't even ride in the same car as you."

"You'll still embarrass me."

"With whom? The deaders?"

"Okay." Kiera added too enthusiastically. "I'm riding with Chris."

Miriam sighed and rolled her eyes.

"See, you're embarrassing me."

"What did I do?"

"Enough," said Chris. "Kiera can ride with me. Anyone else want to join us?"

No one took him up on the offer.

"Okay. I'll lead since I know where we're going." Chris headed for the Ram with the caved in passenger door and patted the side of his leg. "Come on, guys."

Shithead wagged his tail and ran alongside his master.

Kiera became indignant. "I'm not a dog."

"I didn't mean it that way. But you're welcome to ride with your mother if you want."

Kiera tightened her lips and followed Chris to the Ram.

"No offense," Nathan said to Rebecca. "Are you sure you're up to this?"

"You mean battling deaders?" asked Rebecca.

"Yeah."

"You guys saved me from those assholes. I want to help out any way I can."

Alissa cut in. "I asked her to join us not to fight deaders but to help find and load up what we need. I can't say no to someone who wants to help. We can use it."

Nathan nodded in understanding and looked to Rebecca. "I didn't mean to insult you. I didn't want you getting in over your head."

"I appreciate that. As I learned back in North Conway, I can handle myself better than I thought."

The beep of a car horn turned their attention to Chris, who raised his arm and tapped where his watch would be if he wore one. Shithead barked from the back seat. The others climbed into the Land Rover and followed Chris down to the main road.

THE DRIVE TO Gorham lasted less than an hour, taking the group along back roads and through a few small towns with handfuls of deaders roaming the streets, nowhere near enough to be a threat. They stopped once outside of Carroll when they came across a red Toyota SR Tundra abandoned on the side of the road with the keys left inside. Nothing was wrong with the pick-up so, considering the group needed to eventually swap out the banged-up Ram, Alissa jumped in and commandeered it, falling in behind the others.

As the convoy entered Gorham from the west, passing through the residential neighborhood, they found the town deserted. No signs of life. No deaders. Not even indications of a panic or a retreat. It seemed as if the residents had packed up and moved out, admittedly a much better fate than what had befallen almost every other city and town they had encountered.

Chris stopped when the road they were on ended at Route 16, the main road through town. After not moving for several seconds, Alissa pulled the Tundra out of line and drove up beside the Ram, lowering her window and motioning for him to do the same.

"What's up?" he asked.

"That's what I wanted to ask you. Why are we stopped?"

"My fault." Kiera raised her hand but kept her attention focused on the map resting on her knees. "Trying to figure out if we should go right or…." She paused a moment, glanced up, and pointed. "Left."

"You sure?" asked Chris.

"Positive."

"You lead," called out Alissa and rolled up her window.

Chris turned left, followed by the Land Rover and the Tundra.

After a few minutes, Alissa saw their destination on the left: Breen's Farm Supply and Hardware. Judging by the line of tractors and oversized farm equipment parked out front, they had come to the right place.

However, Chris didn't turn into the parking lot but continued along Route 16.

Nathan's voice came over the radio. *"What are you two doing? We just passed Breen's."*

"I know. There's something up ahead I want to check out first."

A few seconds later, the Ram came to a stop and Chris and Kiera jumped out and ran ahead. The others climbed out of their respective vehicles and joined them, ready to engage a pack of deaders or another gang. Instead, Chris and Kiera were circling a military Humvee painted in a mottled-green camouflage pattern parked along the shoulder with the doors open. The others watched. The scene reminded Alissa of her elementary school niece and nephew rummaging through the presents on Christmas morning, a pleasant thought that instantly soured her mood.

"Stop acting like a kid," called out Nathan.

Kiera starred at him blankly. "I'm only fourteen."

"I wasn't referring to you."

If Chris heard, he paid no attention. After checking the tires to insure they were inflated, he scanned the interior for deaders and, seeing none, slid in behind the steering wheel and started the Humvee. The engine roared to life. From force of habit, Alissa scanned the surrounding area, relieved to see the noise attracted no deaders.

As the others approached, Chris leaned out of the cab, a Cheshire cat-like grin on his face. "It works. And it has a full tank of gas."

"Can we keep it?" asked Kiera.

"We?" Miriam dripped with a disapproving mom tone.

Nathan shook his head. "That thing is a gas guzzler. It'll be a monster to feed."

"So are the Ram and the Tundra," argued Chris. "This is impervious to deaders."

"I hate to admit," said Alissa. "He's right. The Ram we stole from Dickson took a lot of punishment. I say we take it."

Nathan turned and headed back to the Land Rover. "You're the boss."

Chris pumped his fist. Kiera responded with, "Fucking A."

"Kiera! Language."

Even being chastised by her mother didn't dull Kiera's enthusiasm.

"Can one of you drive the Tundra?" Alissa asked.

"I will," responded Rebecca as she headed for the pick-up.

Five minutes later, they were parked outside of Breen's, with the Ram and Tundra backed up to the main entrance.

Alissa walked up to the doors, the Mossberg in her left hand. She tried them. They were locked.

"Now for the moment of truth."

Clutching the Mossberg in both hands, she used the stock to smash away the glass and stepped back, waiting for a horde of deaders to rush them. Nothing appeared.

Alissa moved over to the door and peered in. "Hello. Is anyone here?"

Silence.

She cautiously stepped through the door, unlocked them, lifted the upper and lower security bolts, opened the twin doors, and pushed down on the stoppers to keep them in place. Nathan stepped forward and used his boot to clear away as much of the broken glass as possible.

Alissa handed Miriam one of the radios. "Stand guard and let us know if you see anything or anyone."

"Gotcha." Miriam moved to the front of the pick-ups.

"The rest of us, make this quick."

Nathan and Chris were already inside the store searching for what they needed to fortify the compound: portions of chain link fence, barbed wire, a pair of post hole diggers, cement, and any tools they would need. The store had no electricity, so they had to work in the dark. Fortunately, enough sunlight flowed in from the front windows and the skylights so they could work. Alissa, Kiera, and Rebecca spread out and checked the store for any undiscovered dangers. Finding none, they returned and helped bring the supplies out to the trucks.

On their fifth trip outside, Rebecca struck up a conversation. "I didn't expect things to be so quiet."

"Dammit," blurted Alissa.

"What did I say?"

"Sorry, I'm a nurse. If you use that word on a shift then usually all Hell breaks loose."

"I didn't know," Rebecca apologized.

"It's not your fault." Alissa embraced Rebecca. "You can take the nurse out of the hospital, but you can never take the hospital out of the nurse."

"Are we disturbing anything?" asked Chris as he and Nathan carried out two gates for the fence.

"You wish," replied Alissa, releasing Rebecca. "Are we all set?"

Nathan placed his gate by the bed of the Ram. "Almost. Kiera's looking for rope or ratchet straps to secure the items and we're about to load the trucks. We should be ready in a few minutes."

"I'd like to check in back for more barbed wire," added Chris.

"Don't we have enough?" asked Alissa.

"Barely. It's always good to have extra handy in case we need to repair the fence."

"We can do that." Alissa motioned to Rebecca. "Come on. It'll only take a minute."

Alissa led the way to the backroom, pausing at the swinging double doors. She pushed one of them open a few inches and called out.

"Is anyone in there?"

No response.

Alissa raised her Mossberg and entered the storage room. Rebecca stayed close.

"I can barely see a thing," said Rebecca. "Are there any emergency lights?"

"If there are, the power would have been drained by now." Alissa scanned the area, noticing the three bay doors along the rear wall of the building. "See if any of them open. That'll give us plenty of light."

Rebecca headed over to the bay on the right, crouched, and tried the handle. The door didn't budge. Glancing up, she spotted a closed padlock securing the runners to the frame. It was locked. The same with the middle door. The last of the three had the padlock in place but the shackle was not closed. She removed the lock, reached down, and grabbed the handle.

"Looks like we have ourselves a winner."

Rebecca lifted the bay door. Snarls came from the other side. Three deaders stumbled out of an empty trailer parked against the bay, surrounded by a swarm of flies. Rebecca rushed backward and fired two rounds into the closest deader, a male farmer in overalls with a bite mark on its neck. The three bullets blasted into its chest, punching open wounds that oozed congealed blood, doing nothing to stop it. Raising the barrel, she fired again. Her aim was off. Two rounds missed and the third blew off the left side of its face. The farmer deader lumbered toward her, half its lower jaw dangling by ligaments attached to the right side of its skull.

Alissa reacted the moment she heard the snarling. She charged the two deaders to the rear and aimed the Mossberg at the closest, a female in jeans and a red plaid shirt, the right arm stained with blood from a bite wound. Alissa fired. The round tore its head apart, spraying the deader behind it in gore. Before it hit the floor, she switched aimed to the second one, a teenage girl in a Dunkin Donuts uniform with a bite wound on its lower arm. A second round caught it in the jaw, shattering the head. The corpse collapsed. Alissa spun around to check on Rebecca.

The farmer deader lunged at Rebecca, grabbing for her shirt. She moved backwards, trying to put distance between herself and the deader, and aimed the FAL. It grabbed the barrel as she fired, deflecting the shot, and attacked. Rebecca tripped over a pallet and toppled over, landing on the wooden structure, knocking the wind out of her. The deader fell on top of her. She held up the battle rifle, slamming it against the deader's chest and preventing it from getting to her. She wouldn't be able to hold it back for long.

Alissa ran over. She could not shoot the deader without

hitting Rebecca. Spinning the shotgun around, she battered the stock against the back of its head. It ignored her, having worked itself into a frenzy. Alissa looked around for another weapon, her eyes falling on an axe mounted on the wall by the fire extinguisher. Slinging the Mossberg over her shoulder, Alissa removed the axe, rushed back to Rebecca, and drove the blade between the deader's shoulder. That caught its attention. She attempted to remove the blade. It was imbedded two inches into its body. As the farmer deader climbed to its feet and spun around, Alissa unslung her shotgun. Before she could aim, it attacked. Alissa jumped back to get out of the way.

Three gunshots echoed through the storage room. The deader's head exploded. Chris approached, aiming the still smoking barrel of his FAL at the corpse. Nathan rushed up to Alissa and embraced her.

"Are you okay?"

"I'm fine." Alissa hugged him back, holding it for several seconds.

Chris kept the FAL raised and ready to fire. "Were you bit?"

"No." Alissa let go of Nathan and rushed over to Rebecca. "Sorry."

"Don't apologize. You saved my life."

Alissa helped Rebecca to her feet. "Any bites or cuts?"

"I don't think so." Rebecca checked her arms then ran her hands across her neck and face, grateful to see there was no blood.

Chris moved off, checking the rest of the storage area for any more surprises.

"What happened?" asked Nathan.

"We couldn't see back here, so I had Rebecca open one of the bay doors to let some light in. The only one unlocked opened onto a trailer with those things inside."

"I should've been more careful," Rebecca chastised herself.

"It's not your fault." Nathan patted her shoulder. "Who

would have thought somebody would lock those things in there?"

"I think we found our somebody." Chris stood in the far corner between the bay doors and the restrooms. He waved over the others.

A score of bottled water containers and boxes of food were stacked against the wall. In front of them, seven sleeping bags were spread across the floor. Piled in a *cul de sac* behind stacks of lumber not too far away were bags of trash and a deader corpse, the latter of which had numerous gunshot wounds on its body and a machete cleaved into its skull. Three bodies lay around the living area, all bearing bite marks. One had a .38 caliber wound to its head, one held a .38 caliber revolver in its mouth with the top of its head missing, and the third lay in a sleeping bag, a knife in its right hand and a deep incision along the inner left arm from the palm to the elbow, a pool of blood having soaked the bag. Insects swarmed over the bodies, feeding on the remains. Only now did Alissa notice the stench of the dead.

"What happened here?" asked Rebecca.

"My guess is they were holed up here trying to ride out everything when somehow that one got turned." Chris lowered his battle rifle weapon and pointed it toward the corpse thrown away with the garbage. "It bit them all before they took it out. These three took their own lives rather than reanimate. The others asked to be locked in the truck so they wouldn't hurt anyone once they became the living dead."

Rebecca closed her eyes and mumbled a prayer. When she finished, she headed for the front store. "Let's get out of here."

"Not yet." Nathan made his way through the storage area. "Let's get what we came for."

Rebecca crouched and removed one of the bottles from under the plastic wrapping, opening it and taking a drink. "What should we do with the food and water?"

"We have more than enough," said Alissa. "Leave it. Hopefully, somebody who needs supplies will find it."

Less than half an hour later, they had found five more rolls of barbed wire in the back and loaded them into the Ram and Tundra along with everything else. Alissa climbed into the Ram and started the engine.

Nathan stepped up to the driver's side. "Should we lock up the store?"

"Why bother? We already smashed in the front door."

Nathan nodded. "You lead."

She flashed him a flirtatious smile. "I plan on it."

Alissa pulled out of the parking lot and headed home. Nathan fell in line behind her with the Land Rover, with Rebecca and Miriam following in the Tundra. Chris and Kiera brought up the rear in the Humvee.

Halfway home, Kiera's excited voice came over the radio. *"Oh my God! There's a fifty-caliber machine gun in back with several crates of ammunition!"*

Miriam's stern voice cut in. *"Young lady, don't you dare fool around with that. Is that clear?"*

"Oh, mom. You're the reason why we can't have nice things during the apocalypse."

Alissa shook her head.

Chapter Seven

LITTLE STEVIE SAT at the dining room table with his Nintendo Game Boy when Steve came from downstairs. Archer lay curled up by the patio door, napping in the sunshine.

"What are you doing?"

Little Stevie didn't look up from his system. "Playing video games."

"Why don't you go outside and play with Connie."

The boy grimaced. "She's a girl."

Steve stepped over to the table. "I know, but she's part of the family now."

"Great. I have another sister."

Steve folded his arms across his chest. "Connie is lonely and scared, and she's worried about her brother. If you make friends with her and take her outside to play, it might take her mind off things for a while."

"Do I have to?"

"Do you want me take away your video games?"

"Fine." Little Stevie saved his progress and shut down his Nintendo. "You owe me."

"I don't owe you anything for doing what's right."

With a huff, Little Stevie pushed himself out of the chair and trudged upstairs.

He found Connie with her mother and brother.

"Can I help you?" Diana asked.

"Yes, Mrs. Taylor."

"Please, call me Diana."

"Okay, Aunt Diana. I wanted to see if Connie wanted to go outside and play."

"That's so sweet of you." Diana turned to Connie, who sat on the edge of the bed reading. "Why don't you go with Stevie."

"What about Brian?" she asked.

"He'll be fine. He's resting."

"Come on," urged Little Stevie. "I'll show you the ATV and snowmobile in the garage."

"Really?"

"Sure."

Connie put down the book and ran off with Little Stevie.

Diana called after them. "Make sure you stay close to the cabin. And no going into the woods."

"All right," Connie yelled up, already halfway down the stairs.

The two kids ran outside to play, both so excited they left the front door open.

From his resting place in front of the patio, Archer noticed the open door. He stood, stretched, and went over to investigate. He had never gone outside on his own before. Stopping by the jamb, he cautiously peered around the corner, his head jerking back and forth as he studied the area. The two kids had run off somewhere, so no one was around to yell at him. Being an animal, he had never heard the phrase curiosity killed the cat. Even if he had, it wouldn't have made a difference. An opportunity presented itself that he could not pass up.

Making his way onto the porch, Archer jumped off the side and set off to explore this exciting new world.

Chapter Eight

THE TRIP HAD been going well for Brad and the others. They had traveled through New Hampshire without running into deaders, or at least not enough to pose a significant threat. So far, they had stumbled across enough supplies to keep them alive. The biggest break of all had been finding the horses, which would cut their travel time to Nova Scotia in half. The group had a lot to be thankful for, which is why he felt nervous. He waited for something to go wrong.

Brad tried to convince himself he wasn't a pessimist but a realist. To get to Nova Scotia, they had one major obstacle to cross: I-93, which ran through the center of the New Hampshire. From what he had seen on the news during the early days of the outbreak, all major highways and thoroughfares had been jammed with traffic from those escaping the outbreak and, when the first of the deaders reached these, the rate of infection skyrocketed, turning these roads into arteries that allowed the living dead to rapidly spread across the state. Now they had to cross it.

They had been heading north along the west side of I-93 since morning, staying far enough away from the highway to not attract attention, searching for a good crossing point. Exit and entry ramps were out of the question because they were in populated areas overrun by deaders. Crossing in between these ramps also entailed considerable risk due to the number of living dead roaming the highway and the number of obstacles—abandoned vehicles, guardrails, median dividers—that would slow them down enough to be taken out.

Brad prepared to take a chance and cross the highway, hoping for the best, when he spotted an overpass ahead of him. He ordered the others to stop while he studied the road crossing over I-93 for deader activity.

John and Sheri joined him.

"What's up?" asked John.

"That." Brad pointed to the structure. "Or more appropriately, over. I don't see any living dead and there are no clusters of buildings. I think we found our way across."

"The last road sign we passed said we're near Bethlehem," said John.

Sheri crossed herself. "That sounds to me like a sign from God."

"Then let's do this."

Brad spurred his horse ahead, veering to the left so they could approach the accompanying road from level ground. He paused, checking for deaders and, spotting none, led the group in a gallop onto the overpass. A few of the living dead on the highway noticed them race past, glanced up, and snarled. One tried to follow, tripping over the guardrail and rolling down the embankment. In less than a minute, the group had cleared I-93 and were moving along a back road past an abandoned estate.

John rode up alongside him. "That was easier than I thought."

"Don't jinx us."

"Calm down." John leaned over and squeezed Brad's hand. "We've gotten this far because of you."

"Don't say that!" Brad snapped.

John quickly withdrew his hand. "What's bugging you?"

"Sorry." Brad calmed down. "I can't shake this nagging feeling that everything is about to go to shit."

"That I can understand."

"Thanks. It's still no reason for me to be bitchy."

"Maybe we should find a place to stay for the night." John

motioned over his shoulder. "How about that estate over there. It looks comfortable."

"Too close to the highway. I'd rather we get a few miles farther away first."

"You're the boss."

A few minutes later, they turned onto Route 302 and followed it for several miles until reaching the outskirts of Bethlehem. Brad studied the area. Other than a squirrel that darted across the asphalt and bolted up a tree, he saw no activity. He still had a bad feeling, the same one he had all day. However, the horses didn't seem spooked. If he had to choose between his own paranoia or animal instinct, the choice was obvious. Brad led the group into town.

The town had been looted. Not really looted, Brad corrected himself. Whoever had passed through only took what they needed. The convenience stores and restaurants had been picked clean of food and drink, and the only gas station in town had been drained of fuel, at least judging by the nozzles sprawled across the ground. A few vehicles sat on the shoulders, some with their doors open, a few with luggage around them, opened and picked through, more than likely broken down and left behind rather than abandoned in a panic. The citizens here seemed to have been lucky. Brad wondered what happened to them.

Leaving town, the group came upon the Maplewood Golf Course, the once pristine lawn standing over two feet tall and overrun with crabgrass and weeds. The club members would be pissed to see it this way. Not the horses. They saw the lawn as dinner. Brad's horse moved off the road and into the grass, leading the others with it.

"What's going on?" David asked from the back.

"The horses are telling us they want a break," Tina answered.

"That's fine with me." David shifted in his saddle. "I could use one myself."

The group dismounted and sat or laid down on the shoulder while the horses waded into the grass and indulged themselves. David stepped over to Tina.

"Do you still have that toilet paper?"

"Not much left." She opened her backpack and gave it to him. Three quarters had already been used. "Use it sparingly."

"Gotcha." David walked away a few steps and began to unbuckle himself.

Brad waved his hands. "Whoa. Not cool, dude."

"What?"

"Doing your business right here."

"Everybody shits," David protested.

"We don't want to watch," complained Sheri, pointing toward the golf course. "Go farther in there and do it."

"There's bugs in there."

"Do as I tell you." Sheri spoke firmly, like a mother talking to a bratty child.

"Fine." Clutching the top of his pants in his right hand, David moved farther into the overgrown grass before dropping them around his ankles and crouching.

Sheri removed her Red Sox cap and wiped her forehead "How far are we from Nova Scotia?"

Brad shrugged. "Three weeks, maybe four. At least."

"Shit," mumbled Tina.

"Look on the bright side." John gestured to the horses. "We don't have to walk the entire way. And the weather is getting warmer."

"That's what I like about you," Sheri said with all sincerity. "You try to look on the bright side of everything."

"Thanks. Having a positive attitude had gotten me through a lot of tough times. If I didn't think things would get better, I'd have taken my own life months ago."

"God forbid." Sheri crossed herself.

As if to emphasize the beauty of the day, a wind blew in from the north, rustling the tall grass.

And bringing with it the stench of decayed flesh.

The horses became frightened and whinnied. Brad and the others jumped and grabbed their bridles, preventing them from running off. Tina held onto David's horse.

Brad moved closer to the grass. "David, come on. There are deaders nearby."

David had ripped off several pieces of toilet paper and reached behind him, pausing when he heard Brad. "I can't hear you."

"Move your ass."

"I'm wiping now. Hang on."

"Deaders!" Tina yelled.

David heard that. He finished quickly and stood, pulling up his pants.

A deader rose from the grass where it had been laying a yard to David's left. Sensing food, it crawled over and grabbed his leg, pulling itself closer. David jumped to the side, tripping over his pants still around his knees and falling into the grass. He tried kicking it away but his legs had limited mobility. The deader pulled itself onto him, pinning him to the round. Bending over, it sunk its teeth into David's neck.

No one saw what happened because of the grass. They all heard David scream.

John ran into the lawn to help his friend.

"John, come back." Brad wanted to go after him but needed to keep the horses calm.

John raced across the lawn, scanning ahead of him so he didn't step on any deaders. Upon hearing him approach, the deader rose to its feet, preparing for its next meal. As John got closer, he dodged to the left and swung the axe, catching the deader in the face. Teeth and congealed blood flew across the lawn as it fell backwards. John pummeled its head until the skull cracked, splattering its brain across the lawn. John continued smashing at the thing until it stopped convulsing then checked on David.

John knelt by the body, immediately knowing David was dead. The deader had torn a chunk out of his neck the size of a fist. Blood from the severed artery spurt onto the dirt, leaving David pale. John raised the axe above his head, ready to put his friend out of his misery and prevent him from reanimating.

David's eyes opened. The orbs were milky white. It snarled and sat up, grabbing John on both sides of his hips and pulling him in. Before the man could react, the deader that was once David plunged its mouth into his groin. The teeth tore off a chunk of John's skin and severed his artery. John screamed.

"No!"

Brad rushed into the grass to help John. Sheri surged forward and yanked him by the arm, stopping him.

"Let go of me! I have to save John!"

"He's been bitten. He's already dead."

Brad stopped struggling. Tears poured down his face. Anguish filled his heart as he watched John staggering around the lawn. The thing that was once David climbed to its feet and went after John, still chewing the flesh from his thigh. It attacked John, sinking its teeth into his face until they touched bone. It tore of his face, ripping off his nose and exposing the muscles around his jaw. The two fell forward, the tall grass hiding the feeding. John tried to call out to Brad, his cry becoming a gurgle as blood poured down his throat.

"I... I can't leave him like this," Brad cried.

"If you go in there, you'll only get yourself killed."

"Good." Brad sobbed. "I don't want to live without John."

"Stop that." Sheri slapped Brad, snapping him back to reality. "The rest of us need you."

"John...."

"John would want you to go on."

Brad said nothing, clearly in shock. Sheri helped him into his saddle and then said to Tina, "Get him out of here."

"What about you?"

"I'll catch up in a minute."

Tina mounted her horse and then led Brad away along Route 302.

Sheri mounted hers, taking the reins of the other two in her left hand. She checked the golf course one final time. David and John, or what used to be them, stumbled through the grass toward her, snarling, intent on feasting.

"Peace be with you both. Go with God."

Sheri spurred her horse and followed the others.

Chapter Nine

THE PACK HAD sauntered through the charred remains of the town all night and, by morning, had not found a single thing to eat, living or dead, human or animal. Frustration built up inside of Alpha, though it did not recognize the sensation. Days had passed since the pack had a decent meal, allowing the insatiable hunger to intensify. Alpha knew from experience that at a certain point the urge to feed would override their sense of cohesion. Though Alpha could no longer comprehend time, it remembered an earlier occasion when hunger broke down their structure and the lesser ones attacked the leaders. Two Betas had been devoured before Alpha regained control.

That was the reason it had taken so long to pass through town. Alpha had commanded the pack to search every vehicle they came upon for food, remembering that they had stumbled across many meals this way. Nothing lived in this wasteland. Even the bodies they found, which usually provided some form of sustenance, were charred and inedible. The pack groaned from hunger and moaned its complaints with increasing frequency.

The burnt wasteland ended at a break in the road. Alpha stopped the pack and studied the situation. The road leading to the left contained blackened trees and seared bodies. Plush, green vegetation covered the road branching off to the right, like the woods the pack normally hunted in. A chipmunk raced across the road, ignorant of the swarm of living dead. Even with its limited intelligence, Alpha realized the path to the right offered greater opportunity to find food.

Grunting out a command to follow, Alpha led the pack to the that way.

Without realizing it, they passed a sign, its edges singed and some of the paint peeled away, that read:

Route 302 to I-93

Bethlehem   41 miles

Chapter Ten

A LISSA AND THE others returned from Gorham. She felt the tension drain from her now that they were home. Today had been a close call, mostly because they had let their guard down in the storage area. She chastised herself for not having Rebecca tap on the door first to determine if any deaders were on the other side. If she had, they could have avoided that near tragedy. The group had grown complacent after dealing with so many deaders for so long. Alissa would have to reinforce to everyone, including herself, the need to be more cautious if they wanted to stay alive.

If that wasn't bad enough, Alissa fully expected to be read the riot act by Miriam for putting Kiera in harm's way, even though her daughter had not been in any danger. She would advise Kiera to keep a low profile until Alissa could talk down Miriam and convince her Kiera was a vital part of the group.

As they pulled up in front of the cabin, Diana stepped onto the porch. Little Stevie and Connie joined her, although they stayed in the background. Diana seemed anguished.

Alissa jumped out of the Land Rover and rushed up to them. Diana met her at the bottom of the steps.

"I have bad news."

"Is Brian okay?" Alissa feared he had taken a turn for the worst.

"Brian's fine." Diana paused. "Archer snuck out of the cabin while you were gone."

Panic turned to dread. "A-are you sure?"

"We searched the entire cabin for him. I'm—"

"Did you look for him?"

Diana nodded. "The minute I realized he was missing I searched the entire area but couldn't find him."

Alissa's legs went weak. She sat on the stairs. An empty void formed in her heart, sucking away all emotions. She could not believe it. Her beloved Archer was gone. Dozens of scenarios played out in her mind. Archer getting lost and not being able to find his way home. Or injuring himself and hiding somewhere, scared and alone, calling to her. Or being eaten by a bear or coyote... or, God forbid, a stray deader. Despite her best efforts to remain strong, Alissa cradled her face in her hands and sobbed. Tears flowed down her face.

"H-how did it happen?"

Little Stevie stepped forward. "It's... it's my fault."

"And mine," added Connie.

"We left the door open when we went out to play and we think he snuck out then." Little Stevie broke down and cried. "I'm so sorry. Please, don't hate me."

Alissa raised her head and wiped her eyes. "I don't hate you. It was an accident."

Little Stevie ran over and hugged his aunt. Connie joined them. Alissa cried again.

Miriam stepped up to Alissa. "He'll be back. We had an outdoor cat once that—"

"Archer has never been an outdoor cat," Alissa snapped, channeling her grief into anger. "He doesn't know how to survive out there."

Miriam moved away.

"Sorry," said Alissa. "I didn't mean to yell at you."

"It's okay. I understand."

As suddenly as it had struck her, she tamped down the heartbreak over losing Archer, repressing the pain into the deep recesses of her psyche as she had done with every other negative emotion since this fucking nightmare had begun. Grief morphed into determination. She had faced crises such as this for months and would not let this one get the better of her.

"How long ago did Archer get out?"

"Two, maybe three hours ago." Diana looked to Little Stevie and Connie, who nodded in agreement.

Alissa stood and headed back to the Land Rover, returning a minute later with the Mossberg.

"What are you doing?" asked Nathan.

"I'm going to look for Archer."

"It's getting late. The sun will be down soon."

"Don't you dare try and stop me." The anger in her eyes forced Nathan to back down.

"I'll go with you," said Miriam.

"Me, too," added Kiera.

"I'm game," Rebecca joined in.

"Let me get my gun," said Chris.

Alissa forced a smile. "Thanks, but you don't have to do this."

"We're in this together." Miriam placed her hand on Alissa's shoulder.

Chris pretended to pull a sword from his belt. "All for one and one for all."

Shithead barked.

"What about the supplies?" asked Nathan.

Miriam waved him off. "No one is going to steal them. We can unload them tonight or in the morning."

Nathan sighed and gave in. "All right. Let's split into three groups of two. It'll give us a better chance of finding him."

Alissa and the others set off into the woods to find Archer.

Chapter Eleven

S HERI CAME DOWNSTAIRS and dropped into the recliner in
front of the TV.

"How's he doing?" asked Tina.

"Not good. He's taking John's death pretty hard. He says
he doesn't want to go on anymore."

"Do you think he's serious?"

Sheri nodded. "If he had a gun, I think he might end it all."

"Shit," Tina mumbled. "Why don't we stay here another
day and give him a chance to work through his grief?"

"Here" referred to an old farm and stable not far from the
main road they had come across yesterday after the tragedy at
the golf course. No deaders were around and the house seemed
in good shape. Sheri and Tina had checked it and, once certain
no threat existed, brought Brad inside and set him up in the
master bedroom. Tina put the horses in the stable and gave
them hay and water. Brad had fallen asleep the moment his
head hit the pillow, the trauma over losing John in such a
violent manner draining him mentally and emotionally. He
had slept through the night and well into the morning. When
Sheri had tried to wake him so they could head out, he told her
to go on ahead and leave him behind, a request she had refused
despite his pleading and arguing. He eventually gave in and
went back to sleep while Sheri stayed in his room, keeping a
watchful eye on him. With Brad overwhelmed by grief,
somehow Sheri had become the *de facto* head of the group.

"It'll take Brad much more than a day to get over John,"

said Sheri. "But I agree with you. We should stay here at least one more night. All of us could use the rest. It's not like we're in any danger."

"I checked the kitchen earlier. The water works and there's canned food in the cupboards."

Sheri thought for a moment. She wanted to get as far north as quickly as possible to get out of deader territory, though not at the expense of leaving Brad behind. "We'll spend the night here. I think one of us should stay awake at all times just in case."

"Agreed," said Tina.

"Then it's settled. We'll leave at sunrise." Sheri changed subjects. "I'm hungry. What do we have to eat?"

"Canned chili, Spam, and canned beans."

Sheri laughed. "You start cooking. I'll open the windows."

Chapter Twelve

CHRIS STOOD ON the porch of his cabin, enjoying the morning sun while eating a plate of scrambled eggs and sausage. Beside him, Shithead wolfed down the plate of eggs and sausage Chris had prepared for him, doing so with considerably more slurping. He reached down and scratched the dog's back.

"You're a good boy."

Shithead ignored him, switching his attention from eating to licking the plate clean. Let him enjoy himself, thought Chris. They had a special project planned for today.

The search for Archer yesterday afternoon had been a bust. They had scoured the woods for hours and found no signs of him. Alissa was devastated. When he left the cabin last night, she had gone upstairs to cry herself to sleep. Chris radioed in that morning to check on her. Miriam said Alissa had cried most of the night until she finally dozed off around one in the morning. She had not woken up yet. Miriam added that Archer hadn't returned yet. The group planned on setting up the gate across the access road this morning. Chris told her he had a few things to do but would swing by later to help.

Finishing breakfast, Chris placed his plate on the deck, which Shithead dutifully proceeded to lick clean. While the dog enjoyed his breakfast bounty, Chris took his coffee with him. First, he wanted to check out the Humvee, especially the weapon Kiera had found in back – the Browning .50 caliber machine gun, which had been designed to fit into the ring mount on the Humvee's roof. Even more awesome, included with the Browning were five cases containing twelve hundred rounds each. Chris had no idea why someone would leave such a treasure behind, but he wasn't complaining. After bringing the weapon and ammunition inside and securing them, he and Shithead would set out on their other task.

To find Archer.

Chris gathered up the dirty dishes and placed them in the sink with the others from their last few meals, finished his coffee, and found a place among the pile for the mug. After checking his AK-47 and locking the cabin, he and Shithead headed off into the woods.

Truth be told, Chris wasn't surprised that they didn't find Archer last night. Six people traipsing through the woods making so much noise would have scared him off rather than attract him. If Archer got spooked and ran, it made sense he lost his bearings and couldn't find his way home. Since no one had seen anything dangerous in the area, like wolves or coyotes, the chances were good nothing had attacked him. Chris figured if he and Shithead searched the area by themselves, they had a fair chance of finding Archer, assuming he was still alive and hadn't wandered too far away from the cabin.

The plan was so simple even Nathan could have thought of it. He and Shithead would run a line search pattern from their cabin to a mile or so past Alissa's and back again, with spacing intervals of five hundred feet. They would walk slow, calling Archer's name every few minutes, and pausing for a reply. With luck, they would stumble across him in the woods, lost and afraid, and bring him back. Alissa would be happy, he would be a hero in her eyes, and… well, who knows.

Chris' plans of being the knight in shining armor dimmed with each hour. He found no signs of Archer. The more he searched, the more tired and frustrated he became. At one point, he had stopped calling the cat's name as frequently as in the beginning. They had covered an area at least three miles from the cabin without luck. Even Shithead flopped on his side on a pile of moist leaves and stubbornly refused to move.

"I don't blame you boy." Chris crouched against a nearby tree, removed his canteen, drank a few mouthfuls, and then poured some into Shithead's mouth.

Today had been a waste of time. He began to think that maybe Archer was lost for good, which sucked. That would devastate Alissa. She loved that cat more than anything. Maybe they should continue farther into the woods or extend the search pattern on either side of the cabins. He checked his watch. It already neared one o'clock. His best bet would be to go back and help the others then try again in the morning.

Chris stood. Shithead did the same.

"What do you say, boy? Should we search for Archer to-morrow?"

Shithead barked his response.

That's when he heard a frightened meow echo through the forest. Shithead's ears went up.

"Archer, is that you?"

The frightened meow repeated.

"Go find him, boy."

Shithead headed off in the direction of the sound with Chris following, his AK-47 ready to fire if necessary.

Five minutes later, they emerged into a small clearing. Chris burst out laughing. Someone had set a live trap big enough to capture a raccoon or a rabbit, a cage with a door that closed once the critter had wandered inside. Judging by the spots of rust on the cage's exterior, it must have been set up before the outbreak occurred. Archer sat crunched up inside the cave, his fur dirty and matted, but none the worse for wear. Archer glared at him as if Chris had caused his predicament.

"What an asshole."

Archer meowed.

Well, at least Archer was safe and the problem of how to

get him home had been solved.

Shithead strolled over and placed his nose against the cage. Archer hissed and slapped at him, his paw harmlessly hitting the cage. Still, the dog jumped back. Shithead positioned himself parallel with the cage, raised his right rear leg, and urinated on Archer. The cat hissed at him.

"Serves you right, asshole."

Shithead finished his business and raced over to Chris, his tail wagging. Chris bent over and scratched behind his ears.

"You know better than that."

Shithead smiled and gave him one of those I've-been-bad looks that only a dog could master.

Picking up the cage, Chris headed back to the cabin, with Shithead plodding along beside him after a job well done and Archer complaining the entire time.

Chapter Thirteen

CHRIS REACHED ALISSA'S cabin half an hour later. No one was around. Judging by the sounds farther down the driveway, everyone must be working on the gate. He would hopefully be excused for not helping them because of his heroic deed. Well, at least Alissa would forgive him, and that mattered most. Thankfully, Archer had stopped complaining after the ten minutes.

Chris and Shithead entered. "Is anyone here?"

"Where have you been all day," Miriam responded from the kitchen. She entered the living area. "Everyone else has been busting their... Oh, my God. Where did you find him?"

"He got himself trapped in this cage. That's why he never came home. Where's Alissa?"

"She's upstairs sleeping. She's been depressed all day. I'll get her."

As Miriam raced upstairs, Chris placed the cage on the dining room table. Archer meowed in protest.

A minute later, she heard the two women on the second-floor landing.

"Why won't you tell me what's so important?"

"You'll find out."

Halfway down the stairs, Alissa spotted the cage. "Archer!"

She raced down the stairs and over to the dining room table. Opening the cage, she reached in and pulled him out, holding him tight.

"I'm so glad to see you. I was worried sick that I had lost

you."

"He's back." Little Stevie peered over from the top of the landing. He rushed down the stairs, over to Alissa, and petted Archer's back.

"Why's he wet?" Little Stevie leaned closer and sniffed, then grimaced. "He smells like pee. Shithead, did you do that?"

The dog turned away and glanced casually around the room.

"It doesn't matter." Alissa hugged Archer even tighter. "As long as he's safe."

Chris smiled. He enjoyed seeing her happy again.

Alissa put down Archer, who immediately bolted upstairs to groom himself. She walked over to Chris.

"You found him?"

"Shithead and I did. We've been searching the woods—"

Alissa took his head in her hands and gave him a long, deep kiss.

"Gross," aid Kiera as she and the others entered the cabin, each covered in dirt and sweat, a look of confusion on their faces. Except for Nathan, who seemed crestfallen.

"Get a room," commented Steve.

Rebecca smirked. "Is this what was so important you couldn't help us?"

Alissa's face lit up. "He found Archer."

"Is he okay?" asked Kiera.

"He's fine." Alissa nearly danced with joy.

"Where did you find him?"

"In the woods trapped in a cage."

Shithead whined.

"Okay, *we* found him."

The dog barked his approval.

Steve wandered over, pulled out a dining room chair, and sat down. "Where is he now?"

"Upstairs cleaning himself," answered Alissa. "He's dirty and frightened after his ordeal, and someone pissed on him."

Shithead avoided eye contact with the humans.

"This calls for a celebration," said Miriam. "I'll make pork-chops for dinner, and our furry hero gets his own."

Shithead's tail wagged.

Chapter Fourteen

T HE GROUP HAD set out on their journey to Nova Scotia, but not at dawn as originally planned. Brad had refused to go and demanded they leave him behind. Sheri had spent hours trying to persuade him to come along. Only when she reminded him that John would want him to live and continue did Brad finally relent. He asked for a little time to get his emotions together, which took longer than expected. They did not hit the road until shortly after noon.

Brad rode his horse up to Sheri, who had taken point. "Do you know where we're going?"

"We follow this for a few miles to North Conway then pick up a small back road that heads north into Maine. From there, it's clear sailing to Nova Scotia."

"How do you know all this?"

Sheri reached into her jacket and pulled out a folded map which she held up. "Tina found this last night while going through a desk looking for anything we could use."

"Looks like I left the group in capable hands."

"Thanks, but I'm no leader. I'll gladly pass it back to you when you're ready."

They proceeded without incident until the group came upon a sign that indicated the Mount Deception Camping Area lay off to the right. Five deaders meandered along Route 302 with another thirty or so sauntering through the woods. Upon hearing the horses, they turned to the group, snarled, and staggered toward them.

"Shit," Tina called from the back. "What do we do now?"

Sheri didn't reply. Instead, she spurred her horse forward, running along the right side of the road to avoid the closest ones.

Brad brandished his baseball bat in his left hand and set off after Sheri. Tina followed.

They easily avoided the few deaders on the road, weaving their way around them. One went after Brad. He bashed it in the head with the bat, not hard enough to kill it, only disorient it long enough for them to rush by. Running at full gallop, they passed by the danger. The deaders merged into a pack and stumbled after them.

Turning a bend in the road, they came to a small bridge one hundred feet long crossing the Ammonoosuc River. Halfway across, Sheri brought her horse to a halt. A horde of several hundred deaders blocked their path, many wearing National Guard and police uniforms. The closest ones spotted the group and moaned. As one, the horde surged onto the bridge.

"Fuck," said Tina. "We must have stumbled across a detention center."

Brad checked behind him. The deaders they had passed closed in, blocking the road and cutting off their escape.

"We're screwed," said Sheri.

"Not yet." Brad refused to let his friends be eaten alive. Spinning his horse around, he raced back across the bridge. "Follow me."

At the end of the bridge, Brad maneuvered his horse to the left, around the wing wall, and down the bank into the river, pausing to check on the others. Sheri made it down the slope.

Tina was not as lucky. As the deaders drew closer, her horse became spooked and refused to move, neighing frantically and turning in a circle. Tina released the reins and held the crowbar in both hands, ready to defend herself. The first deader lunged, driving its teeth into the horse's neck. The animal bucked, throwing Tina from the saddle. She fell to the ground with a loud thud, screaming in pain from a broken left leg. Eleven more deaders surged around the horse, knocking it over. Dropping to their knees, they tore into their meal. The rest turned their attention to Tina. She crawled toward her friends.

Brad went to help.

Sheri grabbed its bridle and stopped them. "It's too late for her."

A deader, naked from the waist up and with half its abdomen eaten away, hovered over Tina. Tina lifted her right leg and drove the heel into its left kneecap, shattering the bone. As the deader tumbled to one side, Tina rolled in the opposite direction, crying out from pain. Using a large stone by the path leading to the river, she pulled herself into a standing position and hopped away. A deader in a New Hampshire State Police uniform tackled her, knocking them both to the ground. It went after her face. She screamed for help and held it off. Three more dropped to the ground beside Tina and bit her legs.

By now, the horde had reached the end of the bridge. A few of them went after the easy prey. The rest stumbled down the embankment toward Brad and Sheri.

"Let's move." Brad spurred his horse across the river. Sheri stayed close by.

Once on the opposite bank, Sheri paused to gaze at the carnage across the river. She closed her eyes, unable to bear the sight of the feeding. "Peace be with you. Go with God."

The two followed the Ammonoosuc River until it crossed Route 302 again near Bretton Woods. Seeing no deaders in the area, they climbed back onto the road and continued their journey. Neither spoke for the rest of the day.

MOST OF THE deaders that had chased the two humans did not

make it across the river, either becoming stuck in the mud or washed away by the current. Three made it to the opposite bank, one following the humans and two wandering off into the woods.

Those that fed off the crippled human and her horse did not care about the ones who had escaped. They fought amongst themselves, pushing each other aside to tear off chunks of meat and stuff it into their decayed mouths. One deader, a former college professor, had noticed the escaping humans moving east along the river. Its primitive mind realized that potential food existed in that direction, so it followed. The rest of the horde did the same, more out of habit than any conscious decision.

Within minutes, a horde of over two hundred deaders shambled along Route 302 toward North Conway.

Chapter Fifteen

AFTER DINNER, AS the others stayed in the cabin to rest, Nathan led Alissa down the access road to show her the progress they had made.

The group had put in a hard day. All the pilings had been dug and cemented into the ground and the chain link fences attached, stretching to the edge of the woods on either side so nothing could drive around them. The only portion not finished was the adding of the twin gates, which would be completed tomorrow.

"You got a lot done today. I'm impressed."

"Thanks," Nathan replied unenthusiastically.

"What's wrong?"

"Nothing."

"You're upset because you saw me kissing Chris today."

"It's none of my business."

"You're jealous."

"Fine," snapped Nathan. "I'm jealous. Are you happy now?"

"I was thanking him for finding Archer."

"You seemed to enjoy it." The anger drained from Nathan. "Admit it, you like him."

"Chris is sexy and he has that bad boy element—"

Nathan frowned.

"I'd rather be with you."

"Really?"

Alissa chuckled. "Men."

"What do you mean by that?"

"Nathan, we've known each other since high school, and I know you liked me back then. I thought you knew I liked you."

"I hoped you did."

"Why are all the good men afraid to ask out women?"

Nathan hemmed, offering no answer.

"We're in the middle of an apocalypse. We might not have much longer to live. Now would be the perfect time to be together."

"What if I had asked you out and you weren't interested? I didn't want things to be weird between us,"

"Is this weird?" Alissa moved close to him, placed one hand around his neck, and drew him toward her. Their lips met in a passionate kiss. For a moment, he seemed stunned. Then he kissed back, his tongue sliding across her lips and tongue. His hands slid around Alissa's hips and pulled her into him. She moaned when she felt his hardness and ground against him.

"Do you want to go back to the cabin?" he asked.

"Too many people there." Alissa took Nathan's hand and led him to a nearby tree.

"Out here?"

"You've never done it outside before?"

Nathan hesitated. Alissa leaned back against a tree and, grabbing his ass, drew him against her. They fondled each other through their clothes, Alissa enjoying his erection and Nathan her wetness. Passion turned to lust. She unzipped Nathan's pants, pausing long enough to glide her hands along him, enjoying the feel of his fullness. Unable to hold back any longer, Alissa hooked her hands around her jeans and panties, slid them off, then wrapped her legs around Nathan's waist and pulled him close.

For the next few minutes, nothing existed except the excitement between them.

Chapter Sixteen

A LISSA WOKE UP genuinely happy, the first time she had done so since the outbreak had begun. Last night had been wonderful, the first time she had been with a man since separating from Paul. She was not in love with Nathan. Well, at least not yet. She had needed last night, not only to vent months of pent up frustration, but to be in the arms of someone who cared for her and wanted to be with her. She needed the affirmation that someone viewed her as a desirable woman and not merely a deader killer.

The only downside to the morning came from Archer who basked in the sunlight on the windowsill, glaring at her with more distain than usual because someone occupied his side of the bed.

After their tryst in the woods, Nathan had snuck into Alissa's room after everyone else had gone to bed for a further round of love making, this time slower and more impassioned. He had fallen asleep after they finished and she did not wake him, enjoying his company. Especially now as he cuddled beside her, an arm draped across her bare chest.

Archer meowed.

"Get used to it," she whispered.

"Oh, I can," replied Nathan.

"You're awake?"

"I've been up for half an hour."

"Why didn't you say something?"

"I didn't want to disturb you." Nathan cuddled closer to

Alissa. She became excited by the feel of his naked body against hers.

Nathan gently nibbled on the back of her neck. "Want to do it again?"

"No," she lied. "Everyone is awake."

"How do you know?"

"For one thing, it's a little after nine. And I can hear them downstairs having breakfast."

"Who cares?" He cuddled closer to her, his erection poking at her hip.

"You're a sex fiend," she quipped.

"I'm a man."

"That's what I said." Alissa rolled over and kissed Nathan long and enthusiastically, then threw aside the covers and jumped out of bed before her own libido took over.

"You look even more beautiful in the sunlight."

"You've seen me before in the sunlight."

"Yeah, but not naked."

Alissa blushed and slid on her panties. "I'll get dressed and head down first. You follow in a few minutes."

"You're embarrassed of me." The broad smile on Nathan's face betrayed his true feelings.

"Don't say that, even in jest." Alissa donned the rest of her clothes. "There are kids here and I don't want to give them the wrong impression."

"How are else are they going to learn?"

Alissa leaned across the bed and kissed Nathan again. "Behave."

Archer meowed.

Alissa crossed the room to the windowsill and petted him. He closed his eyes and pushed against her hand. "Yes, I still love you, asshat."

As she opened the bedroom door, Alissa whispered, "Come down in a few minutes. And play it cool."

The others were seated at the table finishing breakfast when

Alissa entered the living area. Chris had dropped by. Shithead spread out in the sunlight coming through the patio doors, taking advantage of the location before Archer showed up and bullied him away.

Miriam glanced up from her plate. "I left your breakfast in the microwave."

"Thanks." Alissa reheated the scrambled eggs and bacon while she poured herself a cup of coffee and then joined the others. Connie stood and gave Alissa her seat.

"Thank you." Alissa sat down.

Nobody spoke.

Miriam finally broke the silence. "Somebody had a good night last night."

"Who?" asked Alissa, praying this conversation would not head in the direction she thought.

"You."

"I have no idea what you're talking about."

"Oh, for God's sake." Kiera placed her fork on her empty plate. "The exterior of the cabin may be a fortress, but the walls are paper thin."

Alissa felt the heat surge in her cheeks and pictured herself turning fifty shades of red.

"Why are you so embarrassed?" asked Connie. "You were only hugging."

Alissa went from embarrassment to confusion.

Diana rubbed Connie's head as she answered Alissa's un-asked question. "I told her that you and Nathan were hugging loudly in your room last night."

Alissa quickly changed subjects. "How are we doing on the upgrades to the compound?"

"We're almost finished." Chris was more than happy to change topics. "We set up the chain link fence yesterday. Steve, Rebecca, and Miriam will finish putting up the gates this morning. While they do that, Kiera is going to help me and Nathan string extra strands of barbed wire behind the cabin.

By tonight, everything should be in place."

"Good work. Sorry I didn't help much yesterday."

Steve waved his hand. "Don't worry about it. You had other things on your mind."

Alissa smiled at the thought of having Archer being brought back to her alive by Chris.

At that moment, Nathan quietly slipped down from upstairs. He tried to, anyway. The minute Nathan reached the bottom of the stairs, Steve applauded. Kiera joined in, not wanting to miss out on the teasing. Miriam gently punched them both in the shoulder. Even Shithead joined in with a bark.

Nathan paused by the end of the table. "What's going on?"

Alissa covered her face. "They heard us last night."

Going with the moment, Nathan jogged in place and pumped his fists over his head like a prize fighter who had knocked out his opponent. Alissa wanted to dig a deep hole into the floor, crawl into it, and bury herself.

Her embarrassment became complete when Connie, wanting to be part of the group, clapped her hands and said, "Yay. Aunt Alissa got hugged last night."

Chapter Seventeen

T HE PACK STAGGERED down the road, moving with greater listlessness than usual, an indication they had not fed sufficiently for days. Even Alpha experienced it – the gnawing hunger that consumed its limited thinking and the stiffness in its muscles that slowed its movement. Alpha craved human flesh. The entire pack did. They needed it as desperately as their once-human forms needed oxygen to survive.

In a process none of the deaders were consciously aware of, the protein from living flesh and organs slowed their decomposition. For some reason unbeknownst to the few scientists who had survived the outbreak, protein significantly decelerated the process of decay. It was the reason the living dead did not rot away within a few weeks. Without protein, deaders would gradually lose their ability to function until the body eventually collapsed. At that point, with no means to obtain sustenance, the muscles would atrophy to the point that a deader could no longer move and would lie immobile until deterioration eventually broke down the body.

The first few months after the outbreak had posed no problems to deaders around the world. Food was plentiful. However, now that the dead far outnumbered the living, finding a meal had become next to impossible. Those deaders that had followed the pack had begun feasting off each other, realizing that the limited protein contained within rotting flesh also delayed the inevitable, although not as effectively as that of the living. So far, despite the moments of cannibalism, the pack had maintained its integrity.

If they did not find food soon, though, Alpha could not guarantee their survival.

BRAD AND SHERI were on guard to the point of being jittery. After so many weeks on the road without running into deaders, he had become overconfident about their chances for survival, which had cost them three of their team, including the love of his life. They stayed on Route 302 and did not try cutting cross country due to the mountain ranges on either side which were too steep to navigate on horseback.

They had stopped for the night at a tire store a few miles back and, after checking for deaders, set up camp inside one of the bays where nothing could see or get to them. Sleep had been impossible after what they had experienced hours earlier so, when the sun rose, they set out early, hoping to reach as quickly as possible the small road north of Conway that would take them to Nova Scotia.

Sheri stopped her horse.

"What's wrong?" asked Brad.

"Do you see that?"

Brad stopped. The bushes along the tree line ahead of them shook, not from wind but as if something were about to emerge from them. His first instinct was to escape. Instead, he waited, wanting to know what type of threat they faced. Sheri had already withdrawn her bowie knife, ready to engage deaders.

A deer poked its head from the bushes and scanned the area for danger. Apparently, it didn't consider the humans a threat because it steppedonto the road. Three fawn emerged from the trees. Brad's horse stomped its foot and snorted. The family darted across the road and dove into the woods off to their left, disappearing into the underbrush.

"Jesus Christ," huffed Brad. Then, to Sheri, "Sorry."

"Don't worry. I said the same thing to myself."

"Did you want to take a break? There's a scenic overlook up ahead."

"No. Let's get out of here. I feel trapped on this road."

Brad did not blame her. Taking the lead, he headed for North Conway.

THE FEMALE BETA scouted ahead of the pack. It wore a biker's leather jacket and pants, both of which were stained from the blood and fluids of its victims. Indentations from teeth marks covered its leather jacket from numerous attempts of deaders attempting to feast on her former human form. Nothing had covered its head and, as such, one lucky deader had feasted off the entire left side of the human's face before the female Beta reanimated, leaving an empty eye socket and an exposed jaw and teeth. That had happened days after the outbreak. Now it paused at the bend in the road ahead of the pack, using the trees as cover as it gazed down the road to its right. Something moved. The female Beta studied them through its one murky eye and rejoined the pack.

Alpha waited for a report. The female Beta motioned around the bend and raised two fingers.

The pack grew agitated. Food approached.

Alpha contemplated the best plan of attack. Turning to the others, it pointed to the two sides of the road and grunted. The pack divided and wandered into the woods, three Betas commanding one group and Alpha and the other two Betas, including the female, the second. They spread out along a two-hundred-foot stretch of road, hid amongst the trees, and waited.

THE HORSES CLOPPED along on the asphalt. Off to their right stood a sign announcing the entrance to the Mount Tremont Trailhead. To their left, Brad heard a river flowing close by.

"Where are we?"

Sheri withdrew the map from inside her jacket and opened it, letting the horse lead. "According to this, we're only a few miles from North Conway and the turnoff to Route 16."

"We're making good time."

Sheri slid the map into her inner jacket pocket. They rounded a bend and continued.

The tree limbs off to their right rustled. Brad thought nothing of it, assuming it was another animal. Then the horse neighed, warning of danger. Before either of them had a chance to respond, a deader emerged from the trees and staggered onto the road. Close to forty others joined it, lining both shoulders of the road to the front and rear. The deaders on either end maneuvered so that they blocked the humans' escape. The pack closed ranks but did not move in for the kill.

Brad refused to wait to find out what they intended. He brandished his baseball bat. The deaders became agitated, swaying from side to side, and snarled. One of the deaders that appeared to be in charge, which wore the soiled and blood-soaked uniform of a New Hampshire State Trooper, moved forward. As it did, the others calmed down. The deader approached, stopping in front of the horses. It pointed to Brad and then to the ground.

"What's going on?" asked Brad.

The deader pointed more forcefully to the ground. The other deaders grew agitated again.

Sheri moved her horse beside Brad. "I think it wants you to dismount."

"Screw that."

Brad kicked his horse in the abdomen. The terrified animal bolted forward, rushing for a gap in the circle. He did not get far. The deaders closed in around him, several stopping the horse while a female deader in a leather jacket and only half a face tried to drag him from the saddle. Brad closed his legs tight around the horse and wrapped the reigns around his left hand. With his free hand, he drove the end of the bat into the deader's face, creating a fracture along its forehead. Others closed in, yanking him off the horse and throwing him to the ground. Brad braced himself to be torn apart. To his surprise, the deaders did not feast, using their presence only to intimidate him.

The deader that had commanded Brad stumbled down the line, stopped in front of Sheri, and gestured for her to dismount. She hesitated.

"Run," yelled Brad. "You still have a chance."

The pack of deaders snarled and inched closer.

Sheri dropped the bowie knife and climbed out of the saddle. A few deaders stepped in to restrain her horse. She leaned back against the animal, frightened of what would happen next. None of them harmed her.

Alpha stepped forward along with the rest of the Betas. The other deaders cleared a path for them. Sheri kept her eyes fixed on the leader, shaking as it drew near.

"Sheri, don't show fear."

One of the deaders hovering over Brad bared its teeth, ending the protest.

Alpha moved to within inches of Sheri, examining her. It sniffed. Good. The other human showed defiance, but this one reeked of fear, fear that would make the flesh and blood taste that much sweeter. The insatiable hunger grew more intense, churning its stomach into a knot.

"P-peace be w-with you." Sheri stammered, not wanting to cry. "G-go with—"

Alpha sunk its teeth into Sheri's neck, savoring the soft skin and the squirt of blood that moistened its parched mouth. Despite Sheri's attempts to remain stoic, she screamed from the pain. Alpha dragged her to the ground. As the leader, this human belonged solely to it.

The others, however, were fair game. The feeding frenzy began. The remainder of the pack ripped apart horse and human alike. Brad's yelling ended abruptly when two deaders chewed out each side of his neck, one taking his vocal cords with it. Being fed off by only one deader, Sheri died much slower, although she did not realize it since she had gone into shock after the first bite.

Chapter Eighteen

NATHAN, CHRIS, KIERA, and Shithead spent the day adding the second and third strands of barbed wire around the cabin. Having strung the first strand several weeks ago, by now they were old hands at this, so the project did not take quite as long as the first time. They began to the left of the compound, running the strand at a height of five feet between trees, a foot above the original. Nathan stretched the wire from tree to tree, wrapping it around each trunk, while Chris followed, hammering two nails above and below the wire to secure it. Kiera tagged along behind them, filling empty cans with enough small stones to sound an alarm if anything attempted to break through. Shithead self-appointed himself to guard duty, making certain no evil squirrels presented a danger to the group.

Once they had made one full circle of the compound, they stopped for lunch. Miriam had prepared each of them a pair of egg salad sandwiches and several bottles of water which she placed in a cooler and loaded with ice packs. The men ate both of theirs. Kiera shared one of hers with Shithead, making a friend for life. Few words had been spoken all morning and tension existed between the two men.

They both knew the tension resulted from Nathan's new relationship with Alissa.

"Can we talk?" Nathan asked Chris, hoping to resolve the situation.

"About what?

"About last night. Me and Alissa."

Chris seemed surprised. "Honestly. There's nothing to talk about."

"Well, I know you like Alissa, too."

"I'd be lying if I said I wasn't a little jealous."

"A little jealous?" Kiera chimed in.

"Okay. A lot. But it's fine. Honest."

"Are you sure?" asked Nathan.

"Yes," Chris replied with full sincerity. "You two have known each other since school while I'm the FNG."

"FNG?" asked Kiera.

"Fucking new guy." Chris chuckled at his own joke. "Besides, you two are right for each other."

"How so?"

"You're friends from way back and you think alike. You two are planners. I'm more of a reaction type of guy."

Kiera grinned. "You mean like shooting up propane tanks to stop a deader horde?"

Both men stared at Kiera.

"I'm not complaining. It worked. And it was pretty cool."

The stares turned into glares.

"Okay. I'll shut up." Kiera drank from a bottle of water.

"Kiera may be a bit vocal in her opinion, but she's right." Chris ignored her when she gave him a thumbs up. "I do tend to charge into things without thinking them through."

"Maybe, but most of us wouldn't be here if you hadn't taken the initiative. What I'm trying to say is, you're an important part of the team and I consider you a friend. A good friend."

Chris seemed surprised.

Nathan nodded. "I know I've been rough on you but that's because...."

Chris understood and didn't press the issue. "I'm cool. It won't affect anything."

"Good." Nathan stood and offered his hand. "Friends?"

"Of course." Chris ignored the hand, instead moving in and wrapping his arms around Nathan, enjoying the uncomfortable expression on his face.

"Gross," said Kiera.

Chris moved aside, keeping one arm wrapped around Nathan. "Do you want in on it?"

"I guess." The speed which Kiera joined the group hug belied her disdainful tone. She held Chris a little tighter than Nathan.

Nathan broke the embrace first. "Let's finish this project and get back to the cabin. I think we could use a drink."

"All of us?" Kiera perked up.

Nathan chuckled. "I think one shot of whiskey wouldn't hurt as long as we don't tell your mother."

The three went back to stringing barbed wire while Shithead resumed anti-squirrel patrol. They hung the last strand at a height of two and a half feet, enough to stop any deaders and still allow small wildlife through. They ran out of barbed wire three-quarters of the way through, leaving a gap along that portion of the compound. Next time they made a supply run, they would pick up more and finish the job.

Chapter Nineteen

ALPHA LED HIS pack west along Route 302. A satiated pack. The deaders had spent hours feeding off the humans and horses, stripping the carcasses clean and leaving nothing but gristle. The feast had done more than curb their hunger. It replenished them, restored their energy. Each had eaten enough for them to go days before the hunger returned and their decaying bodies again suffered from lack of sustenance. Alpha experienced the same contentment that any leader did when it had provided for its pack.

Experience had taught Alpha that following a road would sooner or later lead them to more food, only this time the need was not as urgent. That meant the pack would be more pliable and easier for the Betas to control. Alpha assumed they would eventually come across a former populated area, which usually meant some food remained hidden—

An unusual sound attracted Alpha's attention, something not associated with nature. It raised a hand, halting the pack. The deaders moaned. Alpha raised a finger to its lips, silencing them. The sound came from the clanging of metal. Alpha did not recognize the noise itself, only that it was usually associated with humans. With food. If the living dead experienced emotions, it would have been pleased at its possible good fortune.

Shifting its head to hear better, Alpha determined that the sound came from its left, somewhere up an access road that led into the mountains. Its brain associated it with metal scraping against metal from the broken world that existed long ago. Either way, it needed to be checked out.

Second rule of hunting – send out scouts so as not to endanger the pack. Alpha motioned for the Beta in a tattered Carroll County Sheriff Department's deputy uniform. The lower front portion of its shirt had been torn away when several of their kind had ripped opened its abdomen and eviscerated the human for food. Only a gaping hole remained, showing bits of its spine, with a single strand of lower intestine draped across the front of its trousers. When it joined the leader, Alpha pointed up the access road then lifted its hand to shade its eyes. The Beta grunted its acknowledgment and headed into the woods to investigate.

"I THINK THAT'LL do," said Steve, satisfied with their work.

Rebecca, Diana, and he had finished installing the gates to the chain link fence they had erected yesterday. They had set it up so the gates opened both ways, which would cause less damage to the vehicles if they had to bust through in either direction in an emergency. When completed, Steve wrapped a chain around the inner struts of the gate and secured it with a padlock.

"It makes me feel a bit more confident," said Diana. "Now the deaders can't get to us easily."

"I doubt we'll see many of them. Most were incinerated in the firestorm."

"I'm more concerned about humans." Rebecca could not forget what she had endured while held captive by Dickson's gang. "They could still get through."

Steve disagreed. "They'd have to use a car, and we'd hear that."

"I hope you're right."

"Test it for yourself."

Rebecca stepped over to the gate and shook it. The lock held. To be certain, she slammed her shoulder as hard as she could against the inner struts three or four times. The gate moved a few inches but did not bust open.

"Are you satisfied?" Steve asked with sincerity.

"Yes." Rebecca stepped back, rubbing her shoulder. "Sorry to be paranoid."

"You're not paranoid. I can't begin to imagine what the two of you went through."

She forced a smile. "Thanks."

Steve grabbed his weapon and some of the tools. "Let's head back. It's almost lunch."

The two women picked up their weapons and the remainder of the tools and all three headed back to the cabin. They ran into Nathan, Chris, and Kiera returning from stringing the barbed wire.

"You guys all done?" asked Steve.

"Dad," said Kiera in a typical frustrated teenager tone. "I'm not a guy. I'm a girl."

"It was meant generically."

"Yes," interrupted Nathan. "We used all the barbed wire. There's a small segment not completely covered, but we can fix that next time we go on a run. Is the gate finished?"

Steve nodded. "Nothing short of a mob is getting in here."

"Good." Chris bent over and scratched Shithead behind the ears. "You ready for lunch, boy?"

The dog barked once.

They entered the cabin.

NONE OF THEM noticed the Beta hiding behind the trees, watching their every move. It came across the three humans working on the gate and followed them to the cabin, waiting until they were joined by the others and had gone inside. It then rejoined the pack.

Alpha waited for its return. The deputy Beta described what it had observed, beginning by holding up six fingers and then raising both hands as if holding a long gun. It made a square with both hands and then held them together, swinging them both ways, indicating the humans were inside a structure and had a gate guarding the compound. Once finished, the Beta awaited instructions.

Alpha contemplated the situation. At least six armed humans inside a structure. That did not bode well. Alpha recalled several instances from shortly after its reanimation in which it had tried to swarm food inside a building, none of which ended well. Each attempt had cost the pack most of its deaders and a few Betas, which were difficult to replace. The odds of success with only a few dozen pack members were not good. Besides, they had eaten already and were not desperate. Such a move would be foolish.

Nodding once, Alpha excused the deputy Beta, which fell back into position. Alpha continued along Route 302, leading the pack away from the cabin.

Chapter Twenty

ALISSA HELD BRIAN'S brace in one hand. "How is your pain level?"

"About the same."

"About?"

Brian grunted. "The pain level is a little less than when it first happened, but not by much."

"That's normal. It could be two weeks before the pain lessens significantly."

"Shit."

Alissa turned the cast and checked his fingers for any indication of poor blood circulation. The skin coloring was fine.

"Touch your fingers together."

Brian closed his hand until all five fingertips connected.

"Excellent."

"Will I be okay?"

"In four to six weeks, yes. Though it might ache a bit when it rains or the weather gets cold."

"I can live with that. Thanks for taking care of me."

"My pleasure."

Brian went to pull his arm away but Alissa still held the cast. "Is everything okay?"

"Yes. I need to do one more thing." Removing a pen from her pocket, Alissa signed the cast. Brian read it.

Get well soon
Alissa

"I've never had anyone sign a cast before."

Alissa patted his foot. "Get some rest. It's the best thing for you."

Alissa exited the bedroom and headed downstairs. Chris and Shithead had gone home early. Nathan napped on the sofa. Steve read by the fireplace. Little Stevie and Kiera sat in the chair across from him, playing their Nintendo Game Boys. Miriam, Rebecca, and Diana gathered at the dining room table, a full glass of wine in front of each. Three bottles of wine – a merlot, a chardonnay, and a pinot noir – were opened in front of them.

Miriam tapped the chair beside her. "Join us. We're having ladies' night."

"I'm here." Steve did not look up from his book.

"We'll ignore you," joked Rebecca.

"Same as always." Steve grinned.

Miriam placed an empty wine glass in front of Alissa. "What do you want?"

"Chardonnay to start."

"To start?" Miriam winked at her as she filled the glass with wine. "Now that's my type of woman."

"What should we drink to?" asked Rebecca.

"I know." Alissa raised her glass. "To surviving."

The other three women lifted their glasses, repeated the toast, and swigged their wine.

Diana stared into her glass. "I can't believe I... my family... well, at least me and the kids... survived this long."

Rebecca empathized. "Escaping from Dickson was a miracle."

"Don't take this the wrong way." Diana raised her head. "Even though you were gang raped, you have no idea how bad it was being controlled by that fucking bastard." The vehemence with which she spoke the last two words startled the other women.

"How long were you and your family..." Alissa did not

know how to phrase it. "…held captive?"

"Over a month." Diana stared back into her glass. The others thought she had ended the story and refused to press her. After a few seconds, however, she resumed. "We had ridden out the first several weeks of the outbreak in our home outside of Concord, in a little town called Dunbarton. We lived out in the woods. We had enough food to last for a while and a generator that we switched over to when the power lines went down."

"Preppers?" Miriam asked hopefully.

Diana shook her head. "New Englanders. We'd been snowed in enough times to know it could take a week or more for the backroads to be plowed. Everything went well for a long time. Then a horde of deaders from Concord made their way to our town. We never found out why they wandered away from the city. Not that it matters. One day they showed up in our neighborhood. They attacked and ate our neighbors first, which is the only reason we escaped. We had a Silverado with half a tank of gas. When it ran dry, we walked. A few days later Dickson found us. At first, they were friendly. They gave us food and water and drove us back to the Silverado and filled it with their own gas. Dickson told us that since they helped us, we were part of the team. When my husband protested, they beat him up, gang raped me, and threatened to do the same to Connie if we refused to cooperate. For the next month we lived in that damn pick-up. The only time they let us out was to occasionally use the bathroom and to go into stores searching for supplies. I can't tell you how many times me and my husband were almost killed by deaders. They shot my husband in front of the kids a few days before they picked you up and that asshole Joel." Diana paused. "Sorry. I shouldn't have called him that."

"It's okay," said Rebecca. "He was an asshole. He got what he deserved."

"You were only raped once. It happened every night for

me. They made me do… things I had never even considered. If I refused, they would have turned on Connie. At least my kids are safe."

"Amen," mumbled Rebecca.

Diana's hands shook and her voice grew strained as she relayed her story. Alissa feared she might be on the verge of an emotional breakdown. Archer jumped onto the table, made his way over to Diana, and rubbed his head against her hand. She petted him, a tortured smile piercing her lips.

"That's all behind you now," offered Alissa.

"I know, but I'll never get over what they made me do. I did what I had to in order to protect my children. I thank God every night that we ran into you guys. It's nice to know there are decent people left in this world."

"All for one and one for all," joked Miriam.

Diana's gaze switched between Alissa and Miriam. "I want to thank you for putting your lives on the line for us. I don't know how I can ever repay you."

"You don't have to," said Alissa. "We're all in this together."

A strained silence fell across the table with the only sound being Archer purring as Diana petted him.

"How do you think this will all end?" Diana asked.

"You mean us as a group?" asked Miriam.

"No. This outbreak. Are we going to spend the rest of our lives fighting deaders and struggling day by day to survive?"

"God forbid." Rebecca finished her wine and poured another glass.

"It'll end someday," offered Alissa.

"Are you certain?"

"Yes," said Alissa, only half believing it. "I'm sure someone somewhere is working on a vaccine. Once the government gets back on its feet, they'll probably organize a counteroffensive to take back what we've lost."

Miriam crinkled her brow. "Do you really think so?"

"Yes. Sure, the heavily populated coasts are a nightmare. I know. I was in Boston when this thing hit. But so much of this country is open area and scarcely populated, I'm sure resistance against the deaders is being organized there. I believe... I *have* to believe that, otherwise I couldn't go on."

Another strained silence fell across the table.

Miriam finally broke the tension. "Enough depressing talk." She refilled everyone's glasses and then held up her own. "Here's to drinking too much, getting buzzed, and forgetting our problems for a few hours."

Diana perked up. "I'll drink to that."

NIGHT HAD DESCENDED hours ago, making hunting that much more difficult. The pack relied primarily on its sense of sound and smell but, once prey had been detected, daylight helped them track better. Alpha sensed something unusual. Not prey or another predator. More like the presence of its kind, but in much greater numbers.

South of Bretton Woods, the pack encountered a horde of deaders several hundred strong staggering east. Upon seeing the pack, the horde became agitated and surged forward. The closer they approached, the more they settled down, realizing they were dealing with their own kind.

When both groups were within several yards of each other, Alpha ordered his to halt and stepped forward to meet the newcomers. Several paid no attention to Alpha and his pack, viewing them as other deaders like themselves. Most sensed something different, something special about Alpha, though they could not understand what. When they stopped, Alpha raised its hand for the five Betas to step forward, signifying Alpha was in command. Many within the horde moved back, some confused, some in awe, some wary of the power of this unusual deader.

Alpha pointed to itself and to the Betas then, holding its fingertips together, tapped its mouth. The horde moaned, some deep part of their memories associating the gesture with food. Alpha raised both hands, silencing the horde. Moving back a few paces to join the Betas, Alpha pointed toward the horde then spread its arms to the sides. Again, the horde moaned, understanding they were being asked to join the collective and accept these deaders as their leaders. As one, the horde merged with the pack, most willingly agreeing to serve their new master, several oblivious to the event and merely following the others. Alpha turned and moved to the rear of its pack, the deaders spreading to make a path. Once through, Alpha continued east along Route 302, the horde falling in behind it.

Alpha headed back toward the humans they had encountered earlier today. With a few dozen deaders, the chances of overwhelming the humans were slim. With the increased numbers, victory was certain.

Chapter Twenty-One

"**I**T'S A BEAUTIFUL day," said Miriam.

"It looks cold out." Diana bit into some sausage.

"Right now, it is. I went outside before I made breakfast and the thermometer read thirty-eight degrees. Once the sun crests the trees, it'll probably be in the mid-fifties."

"Still too chilly for me." Rebecca wrapped her hands around the coffee mug to keep them warm. "I'm a summer girl."

Kiera made an exaggerated expression of disgust. "I don't mind the heat but the humidity sucks."

"That's what I loved most about living on Nahant," Nathan chimed in. "No matter how hot and humid the day was, at night you got that ocean breeze that cooled things off. Right, Alissa?"

Alissa smiled and nodded, reminiscing about the good old days.

"What's on the agenda today?" asked Steve. "Are you going to find a dam to burst and then fight deaders in the flood?"

Nathan chuckled. "Don't give Chris any ideas."

Connie's face lit up. "We should have a picnic. Isn't there a spot not far from here where we can see Mount Washington?"

"There is," said Alissa. "It's only a few miles from here."

"Can we do it, mom?" Connie nearly bounced out of her chair.

"I don't know. It could be dangerous."

Connie pouted.

Alissa shook her head. "If we all go, it should be safe. In fact, I think it's a great idea. It'll be nice to get out of the cabin and not do a supply run."

Connie's eyes popped open and she pleaded to her mother, "Please?"

"Okay, I give in."

"Then it's settled," said Miriam. "I'll make sandwiches after we pick up and we'll have lunch there."

Nathan took a sip of coffee. "I'll radio Chris later and see if he wants to join us."

"Then I'll make two more sandwiches."

"One for shithead?" asked Kiera.

"Of course."

Steve stood, picked up his coffee mug, and limped toward the front door. "You all have everything well in hand. I think I'll finish my coffee outside."

Miriam flashed him a loving frown. "You could help with the dishes."

"But all that movement would hurt my leg."

"Don't worry, gimpy," teased Nathan. "I've got this."

"Thanks."

As the others finished their breakfast or cleaned up, Steve headed outside to the front porch.

CHRIS SAT ON the back deck of his cabin, relaxing in a lounge chair while eating his breakfast. He had made himself scrambled eggs and bacon, preparing a few extra strips for Shithead who sat beside him, his eyes constantly moving between the plate and his master. Every few minutes, Nathan held out a piece of bacon that the dog gently took from his mouth and barely chewed before swallowing, then went back to begging for more. When Chris finished breakfast, he placed the plate on the deck and watched as Shithead spent several minutes licking it clean.

It was too nice a day to sit around doing nothing. Once he finished his coffee, he and Shithead would head off and explore the woods beyond the cabins before dropping by Alissa's for dinner.

ALPHA GATHERED THE horde of deaders on Route 302 in front of the access road leading to the cabin where the humans dwelled. The anticipation amongst the deaders was palpable. Rustling and moaning permeated throughout. Thanks to Alpha, they would soon be feeding on warm flesh and tissue.

Alpha raised a finger to its lip, ordering the horde to be quiet so as not to warn the humans. They quieted down. It then summoned two of its Betas, the National Guard officer and the sheriff's deputy. Alpha pointed to the pack and then stretched out its arms, indicating the woods on either side of the cabin. The Betas understood the most basic rule of the hunt. Set up an ambush behind the prey in case the prey ran. The two Betas did not mind leaving the rest of the horde because they knew that once the humans had been captured, all would join in the feast. The two Betas summoned twenty-five deaders each and proceeded into the woods on either side of the horde.

Fifteen minutes passed. The horde grew restless, wanting to eat. Alpha turned to them. They settled down. Raising its left hand, Alpha motioned for them to march. The deaders surge forward, nearly two hundred moving up the access road. When they reached the chain link fence, Alpha gestured for them to push against the gates. The horde obeyed. As expected, the gates bent against the combined weight of the deaders, straining until the padlock could no longer withstand the pressure and snapped. They withdrew a few paces.

Alpha and the three remaining Betas took the lead and led the pack toward the cabin.

Chapter Twenty-Two

S TEVE SAT ON the front porch enjoying his morning coffee while the others cleaned up. It was an exceptional warm day for late February – low fifties with a warm, pleasant sun. Which in New England meant next week they could expect a blizzard or sub-zero temperatures. One of the joys of living in the northeast. If you don't like the weather, wait a few minutes. Part of him understood why so many snowbirds went south—

The clanging of metal from down the access road interrupted his mental ramblings. Placing his mug on the wicker table, Steve left the porch and headed out to see what caused the sound. Most likely some dumb ass deer or bear head butting the fence. Probably nothing to worry about but better to be safe than sorry.

As he approached the end of the compound, a horde of deaders shambled up the road. A deader in an EMT uniform, a large chunk of flesh ripped out of its right cheek and its left arm stripped clean, leaving the bones dangling lifeless by its side, held up its hand as if telling him to stop. Fuck that. Steve limped back to the cabin.

He burst through the front door, locking it behind him. "There are a couple of hundred deaders coming up the access road."

"Fuck!" Alissa ran for the front windows, grabbing her Mossberg from the rack near the door. Nathan and Miriam followed. The others stayed in the center of the room.

The horde approached to within twenty-five yards of the

cabin and stopped. They let out a collective moan until one of the deaders raised its arm. The others stopped.

"What the fuck just happened?" asked Nathan.

"I don't know." Alissa turned the knob on the front door.

"Are you nuts?" asked Miriam.

"I need to see this for myself."

Alissa opened the door and stepped onto the porch. The ravaged deader in the EMT uniform took three steps forward. Alissa raised her shotgun. The horde groaned in unison. The deader pointed to the weapon and then to the ground.

"What's going on?" Nathan asked from inside the cabin.

"I think it told me to disarm."

The EMT deader repeated the gesture and the horde groaned again. Alissa lowered the barrel. The commotion ceased. The EMT deader pointed to the cabin and then waved its hand toward itself.

"It… it wants us to come outside."

"No fucking way." Nathan pulled back the bolt to his FAL.

When Alissa did not respond, the horde groaned again. The EMT deader held up two fingers.

Nathan stepped up behind Alissa. "Did that thing tell us we have two minutes to respond?"

"I think so."

"What are we going to do?"

"Fight!" Alissa raised her middle finger to the deader and went back inside, locking the door behind her. "Miriam, check out back and see if there are any deaders there. Diana, get the kids and be ready to evacuate when I tell you. The rest of you, arm up. Where's the radio?"

Kiera took it from the mantle and brought it over. "What are you going to do?"

"Ensure we survive." Alissa keyed the talk button. "Chris, are you there?"

An agonizing few seconds passed before he answered. *"What's up?"*

"No time to chat. We have a couple of hundred deaders about to attack the cabin. We're going to make a break for it. Get out of there while you can. Take the Humvee to a safe location and wait for us to call you. We'll need you to pick us up. Don't call again until you hear from us. Out."

Alissa shut off the radio and stuck it under her shirt. She peered out the window again. The EMT deader had rejoined the horde.

Miriam raced up. "Nothing out back that I could see."

"Good. Let's get ready to bug—"

As she watched, a deader dressed like a college professor raised its hand and dropped it. The horde snarled and attacked, breaking into three waves, each led by a Beta. The main wave followed the EMT deader onto the porch while the other two broke right and left, commanded by the New Hampshire State Trooper and female biker Betas, respectively. Within seconds, they had surrounded the cabin.

"No time to chat. We have a couple of hundred deaders about to attack the cabin. We're going to make a break for it. Get out of there while you can. Take the Humvee to a safe location and wait for us to call you. We'll need you to pick us up. Don't call again until you hear from us. Out."

"Alissa! Alissa!" No use. She had turned off the radio.

Shithead stood by him, sensing the tension.

"Come on, boy. We gotta move."

Chris grabbed his AK-47 and a bag of spare magazines and raced out of the cabin, with the dog close on his heels. He opened the Humvee's passenger door. Shithead jumped into the seat. Chris placed the AK-47 and the bag of magazines on the floorboard then shut the door. Heading back inside, he gathered up the five cases of belt ammo and placed them in the back seat of the vehicle. Going back once more, he retrieved the .50 caliber machine gun. Chris attached the weapon to the ring mount, lifted the cover, and loaded the first belt of ammunition into the feed tray. Pulling back on the bolt, he fired three rounds. Thank God, it worked. He closed the cover over the belt.

Chris slid into the driver's seat and started the engine.

"Get ready, Shithead. It's slaughtering time."

DIANA REACHED THE top of the stairs and burst into their bedroom.

Brian pulled on a pair of pants. "What's going on?"

"We're being swarmed by deaders. Two hundred of them."

"How are we going to fight that many?"

"We're not. We're abandoning camp. Hurry."

"Shit." Brian slipped on his sneakers without bothering with socks.

Diana glanced around the room. "Where's your sister?"

He pointed to the room beside them at the far end of the hall. "Playing with Little Stevie,"

Diana barged out of the room and down the hall, startling the kids when she rushed through the door.

"Mom, you scared—"

"Come with me. We're under attack and have to get out of here."

Both children obeyed without argument. They met Brian by his door and rushed to the landing.

"Wait!" Connie spun around and ran back down the hall.

"What are you doing?"

"Getting Archer."

Diana tried to grab her arm but missed. "We don't have time."

Little Stevie took off after Connie. "We're not leaving Archer behind."

"Fuck!" Diana kicked the wall then spun around to face her son. "Don't you move from this spot."

"Yes, ma'am."

Diana ran after the children.

CHRIS REACHED THE end of the access road to his cabin and swung the Humvee so fast onto Route 302 that the back end fishtailed. Shithead barked excitedly. Chris eased his foot off the gas until the vehicle corrected itself and then accelerated, hoping he was not too late.

ALISSA AND NATHAN opened the door and stepped onto the front porch. Kiera and Steve unlocked the windows at the corners of the living room, lifted the pane, and punched out the screen with the stocks of their weapons. The four blasted away at the horde, taking down a dozen deaders, not nearly enough to stop the onslaught. When the first deader reached the porch, Alissa and Nathan headed inside and closed the door. Kiera and Steve slammed shut their windows.

A second later, scores of dead hands pounding on the front façade echoed through the room.

Miriam joined them. "They've surrounded the cabin on both sides."

"Fuck," said Nathan.

"What about the kitchen door?" asked Alissa.

"It's blocked by deaders."

Kiera scanned the room for another means of escape. "How are we going to get out?"

"Is there an attic?" thought Steve.

Alissa shook her head. "Even if there was, we'd still be trapped in here and surrounded on all sides."

The windows along the front of the cabin shattered. Dead hands reached through, oblivious to their skin being shredded, groping at the food inside. Nathan and Steve headed for the windows, shooting every deader they saw.

"Then this is the end?" Kiera seemed ready to cry.

Alissa refused to go down without a fight. "We'll distract them on the porch and hopefully attract the ones on the sides. Miriam, you and Diana get the kids to safety. We'll follow once you're in the clear."

"Gotcha." The expression in Miriam's eyes indicated she knew they would not survive the next few minutes.

A large crack snapped its way down the length of the front door. The hinges strained under the weight of the mass of dead and gave way. The door tumbled onto the floor, allowing deaders to swarm inside.

CHRIS GUNNED THE Humvee up the access road to Alissa's cabin and hit the brakes once inside the compound.

"Jesus fucking Christ."

Shithead whined.

Shifting into park and leaving the engine running, Steve crawled up through the opening. He swung the machine gun to face the horde. Firing straight into them meant stray rounds could go flying through the cabin, so he lowered his aim and squeezed the trigger. A stream of .50 caliber rounds tore through the rear line of deaders, ripping off their legs. Their crippled bodies fell to the ground. He slowly moved the machine gun back and forth across the line, dropping more and more of the living dead. Once the deaders to the rear had fallen, he took out the second, third, and fourth line. By the time he had expended the ammunition in the first case, nothing but a mass of moving flesh remained in front of the cabin.

To his horror, he saw that the front door had collapsed and other deaders staggered into the cabin.

ALISSA AND THE others fired at the deaders, dropping the first twelve that came through the shattered door. They created a mound of dead flesh that slowed the others behind it. A few pushed through and tripped over the pile, falling to the floor. Nathan and Steve stepped forward, finishing them off with a double tap to the head. Flies and wasps displaced by the gunshots swarmed through the living room.

They heard the kitchen door break off its hinges accompanied by the groans of deaders. Alissa and Miriam raced over to the doorway. Deaders rapidly filled the kitchen. The two women fired into the pack.

"Someone get the dining room table."

Kiera ran over, threw the chairs aside, and pushed the table across the hardwood floor until it blocked the door. Pressing their weight against the table, the three fired at the deaders in the kitchen but could not stem the tide. The pack reached the table and started to push it out of the way.

ALPHA MOANED AT the Humvee in anger, an emotion it no longer recognized. It had not counted on this human having so much firepower. It remembered others in similar vehicles using such weapons with devastating results on others of its kind. This human needed to be taken out quickly.

Raising its head, Alpha issued a loud, prolonged groan, ordering the State Trooper and female biker Betas to bring their packs into the fight.

ON EITHER SIDE of the cabin, the less experienced deaders heard the commotion out front, their primitive minds associating it with food. Most turned and stumbled back toward the noise.

To the left, the female biker Beta heard its master's command but ignored it. The deaders that broke rank would satisfy the need. It refused to allow this prey to escape. It groaned, attracting the attention of the experienced deaders. They faced their leader. The female biker Beta directed half to form a line along this side of the cabin and the rest to go around back.

The State Trooper Beta did not hear Alpha's command. It directed the attack through the kitchen.

DIANA FOUND CONNIE trying to get Archer from under the bed where he hid, terrified by what went on downstairs. Little Stevie had retrieved the cat's carrier and placed it on the bed.

"Leave the damn cat."

"No!"

Diana stepped into the bedroom and grabbed Connie by the arm. "We don't have time."

"Aunt Alissa saved our lives." Connie broke away from her mother and rushed back to the bed. "I'm not going to let her cat die."

"Shit," Diana mumbled. Going over to the bed, she helped her daughter retrieve Archer.

The cat would not budge.

Little Stevie laid on the floor and called to him. "Come on, buddy. We have to go."

Archer meowed.

"It's okay."

Archer inched forward into Little Stevie's hands. He gently pulled the cat toward him, lifted it into his arms, and placed it in the carrier. Diana slammed the top lid shut, scaring Archer, and locked it. She picked up the carrier and headed for the door.

EVERY TIME NATHAN and Steve paused to reload, more deaders pushed through the front door, enough that they could not stop them all. Both men fell back, each grabbing a saddle bag of spare magazines.

The flood in the kitchen became too much for the women to hold back. The table pushed across the floor, allowing a few into the living area. Alissa and Kiera shot each in the head as Miriam attempted to hold the table in place. They could only delay the inevitable.

DIANA REACHED BRIAN and pushed him down the hall.

"We have to get out of here—"

A dozen deaders had already forced their way into the house and were pushing the others toward the back deck. More entered as she watched, those from the kitchen closing in on the stairs.

"Come on." Alissa waved for Diana and the kids to join them.

Little Stevie attempted to push past but could not get around Diana, who was frozen by fear.

The deaders from the kitchen reached the bottom of the stairs.

"Hurry or you'll be trapped!" screamed Miriam.

Kiera broke free from the others and jumped onto the stairs. A deader, naked from the waist up and with one arm torn off, lumbered after her. Kiera placed the barrel of her shotgun against its face and fired. Its head exploded. Seven deaders followed as Kiera backed up the stairs.

"What are you doing?" Miriam seemed on the brink of losing it.

"I'll take care of Stevie and the others. You and dad get to safety."

Before anyone could respond, two things happened. First, Kiera shoved Diana back down the hall toward the bedrooms at the rear of the cabin.

Second, a pack of deaders surrounded Alissa and the others.

CHRIS DUCKED BACK into the Humvee for his AK-47 to go

help those in the cabin when Shithead barked. Another fifteen or so deaders emerged from the left side of the cabin, heading toward him. He retrieved a full case of ammunition, climbed up into the mount, switched it out with the empty one, and pulled back the bolt on the machine gun. Nothing behind the pack would suffer from friendly fire, so Chris swiveled the machine gun toward them, raised the barrel, and squeezed the trigger. The rounds ripped apart the deaders, creating a cloud of blood and gore as the gunfire churned the pack into a pile of tattered flesh. Chris released the trigger. Nothing moved. Not much remained to move.

However, deaders from the pack in front of the cabin crawled toward the Humvee. Swinging the machine gun in their direction, Chris fired. The bullets chewed up chunks of body parts and organs, splashing them against the porch and cabin. When the belt ran out, all the deaders had been butchered except those inside. A pool of congealed blood oozed under the bodies and toward the access road.

Chris climbed back into the Humvee cab, retrieved his AK-47, and patted Shithead.

"You stay here, boy. I'll be back."

Jumping out, he closed the door behind him and ran across the compound toward the cabin.

ALISSA SLID ASIDE the glass door to the back deck. "This way."

Miriam joined her, taking a last glance at the staircase to see if Kiera was safe.

Alissa pointed to the opposite end of the deck. "See what's down there."

As Miriam rushed over to the rail and peered over, Nathan, Rebecca, and Steve exited the cabin, the former sliding the door closed behind him. They backed up, keeping their weapons trained on the deaders approaching from the other side.

"We're not going to be able to hold them for long," warned Steve.

Miriam scanned the area around the deck. "It's clear."

"Then let's get out of here."

Alissa sat on the railing, swung her legs over the side, and jumped the ten feet to the ground below. She hit the dirt and rolled. Groaning came from under the deck. Half a dozen deaders, the ones the female biker Beta had sent around back, lumbered toward her. She retreated into the woods, putting as much distance between herself and the living dead as possible. Raising her Mossberg, she took out two of the deaders before she ran out of ammunition. She had no time to reload. Swinging the shotgun around, Alissa braced herself to bash in the deaders' faces with the stock.

The heads of the last four exploded in succession. When she looked up, Nathan, Miriam, Rebecca, and Steve stood by the railing, smoke rising from the barrels of their weapons.

"Thanks." Alissa motioned for them to join her. "It's all clear."

Rebecca jumped first, tripping and landing on her hands and knees. Nathan climbed over the railing and dropped to the ground, then slung the FAL over his shoulder.

"Come on, Steve. I'll help you."

Steve sat on the railing, lifting his leg over the side.

The glass in the sliding doors shattered. A pack of deaders pushed their way through and lunged at Steve and Miriam.

KIERA STOOD AT the top of the landing, blasting apart each deader that ascended the stairs. Bits of flesh and organs and puddles of congealed blood covered each step, making the ascent difficult.

"Go to Aunt Alissa's room. I'll be there in a minute."

Kiera paused to reload. The deaders pushed past the bodies on the stairs and swarmed onto the landing. Kiera raised her

Mossberg and fired directly into the face of a deader in an Army uniform, its neck chewed out, revealing its ravaged larynx. Its head exploded, splattering Kiera and the walls in gore. She moved backwards down the hall, lining up her shots, taking down the approaching deaders one bullet at a time. When the Mossberg had expended its rounds, Kiera gave the remaining deaders the middle finger and rushed into Alissa's bedroom, closing and locking the door behind her.

Diana and the kids appeared on the brink of panic. Only Brian remained composed.

"What can I do?"

"Help me push the bed in front of the door."

The two teenagers dragged the bed away from the wall. Little Stevie and Connie slid into the open space and, together, the four of them pushed the heavy piece of furniture against the door. Dead hands began banging and scratching on the other side.

"Do we have any other guns up here?" asked Kiera.

Diana shook her head.

"Shit." Kiera reloaded the Mossberg and checked the bag. She had enough to reload once more. Then they were screwed.

CHRIS BURST INTO the cabin expecting to find half his friends dead, or worse, reanimated. Thank God he did not find that.

A swarm of deaders busted through the glass doors leading out on the deck and went after Miriam and Steve.

Moving to the side so his friends would not be in the line of fire, Chris raised the AK-47 and emptied the magazine, dropping or crippling a dozen deaders. A few turned and lumbered toward him, leaving only five still converging on his friends. Hopefully, they could handle that number.

A hand reached out and clutched at his hair. Chris jumped aside. He had not noticed the pack heading up stairs. Seeing new prey, seven of them descended.

Retreating to the front of the cabin, he switched out an empty magazine for a full one. Taking careful aim, he took out the deaders one by one with head shots. Bodies covered the living room floor. Chris slipped on a chunk of lung, toppling over backwards. His shoulder slammed against the hard wood. Pain shot down his right arm but, thankfully, he had not broken any bones. Seeing its opportunity, an obese, topless female deader, its chest and breasts stripped of flesh and tissue, attacked. Chris fired six rounds without aiming. The bullets ripped into its chest, bursting open its abdomen and stomach. Undigested body parts slid from its ruptured stomach, dropping to the floor with a sickening plop. The deader slipped on the pile and crashed face first onto the hardwood, shattering its face. A God-awful stench of decay and bodily gases washed over Chris, making him wretch. Chris crawled to a clean portion of the floor and got to his feet.

As the others drew closer, he withdrew out onto the porch, firing at each that emerged in the open doorway. When his semi-automatic ran out of rounds, he retreated again, reloading in the process, then finished off the last of the deaders pursuing him.

Not realizing Diana and the kids remained trapped upstairs, Chris raced around to the left of the cabin to help those escaping off the back deck.

ALPHA GROUND ITS decaying teeth. This attack had not gone according to plan. They should be feasting by now. These humans were not like the others they had encountered. These were heavily armed and fought back. It wanted to attack this one human and take him down, slowly tearing him apart and making him suffer for what he had done to the pack. However, self-preservation prevailed. Doing so would only get itself killed. It would deal with this human later.

Alpha headed into the woods and circled around to the

rear of the cabin to coordinate the hunting of any humans who might have escaped, then organize another push to swarm the cabin.

THE DOOR TO the bedroom cracked. Diana and Brian rushed over to the head of the bed and pushed against it with their shoulders, a futile gesture that would buy them seconds at most.

Kiera knew they had to find a way to escape. And fast.

She stepped over to the windows facing to the rear. She saw a small slanted roof six feet in width and running along the side of the cabin. If they could get out there, they should be okay. Unhooking the latches, she lifted the pane and pushed out the screen.

"Come on. We should be safe out here."

Little Stevie and Connie ran over, the latter holding the cat carrier. Archer sat inside, hissing at everyone. Kiera helped Little Stevie out the window.

"I'm scared," he said.

"You'll be fine." Kiera responded in her most calm voice which belied the adrenaline pumping through her system. "Don't stand up and carefully crawl to the end."

Little Stevie did as he was told. Kiera took the carrier from Connie and placed it on the floor. "Now you. Do the same thing. The deaders can't get you out here."

After Connie climbed out, Kiera placed the carrier on the roof, roof, holding the handle so it did not slide off, and pushed it toward Connie. "You two are going to protect Archer. Don't let go of the carrier."

"I promise I won't."

The weight of the deaders outside the door became too great. The door snapped open and pushed the bed aside a few feet, allowing the living dead into the bedroom.

STEVE HAD BEEN sitting on the railing getting ready to jump when the deaders broke through the sliding glass doors. He needed no further encouragement. He dropped from the deck, favoring his good leg when he hit so as not to do further damage to his wounded one, and praying he wouldn't break or sprain anything in the process. Steve hit the ground and collapsed, rolling onto his back. His pump action shotgun slid off into the woods.

Alissa rushed over and helped Steve to his feet. "Are you okay?"

"Yeah." Steve grunted as he stood. "But my shoulders will hurt in the morning."

Once Steve had jumped, Miriam sat on the railing and swung her legs over the side. The EMT Beta lunged, hoping to catch the human before she got away. It grabbed her shoulder and wrist and bit down, locking its teeth around her upper arm, sinking deep into the leather jacket. Miriam involuntarily pulled away, falling off the deck and pulling the Beta with her. The two crashed onto the ground, knocking the air from Miriam's lungs. The Beta rolled to the side, scrambled onto its hand and knees, and attacked.

Nathan ran up and kicked the EMT Beta in the face before it could bite Miriam. Several decayed teeth shattered and flew out of its mouth. The deader fell onto its side. As Alissa pulled Miriam to safety, Nathan raised the FAL to fire. The Beta crawled to its feet, ducked, and rushed Nathan. The bullets sailed harmlessly over its back. Its shoulder connected with Nathan's chest. The two tumbled to the ground. Nathan had enough foresight when he fell to place the FAL across his chest and slam it into the deader's neck, preventing it from falling on and biting him. The Beta desperately snapped at Nathan's hand.

It would have succeeded if Alissa had not run over to help Nathan. Clutching the deader by the hair, she yanked its head back at the last moment. Its teeth closed on air. The Beta jerked its head to the side. Its hair came out in a clump in Alissa's hand. As it attempted to bite Nathan a second time, Alissa grabbed it by the forehead, digging her fingers into its eyes. Nausea welled up in Alissa as her fingers plunged into the gooey orbs. At least she kept the deader's head immobile. It howled and snapped its teeth, hoping to bite flesh, Alissa withdrew her Glock from its holster, placed the barrel against the EMT Beta's right temple, and fired three rounds. Its head exploded, the only part remaining being the lower jaw and the portion of skull from around the eyes she clutched in her hand.

Alissa tossed the remains aside and knelt beside Nathan, checking his hand.

"Did it bite you?"

"I'm fine. Just a bit rattled."

Alissa embraced him tight.

"Miriam, what about you?" asked Alissa.

Miriam pulled the leather jacket down over her right arm and examined where she had been bitten. "It didn't break through."

"Thank God," said Alissa.

"We better get moving," said Steve, pointing to the two sides of the house. Four deaders rounded the corner to their right and eleven more to their left.

The humans set off into the woods.

THE STATE TROOPER Beta heard the machine gun fire out front, followed a minute later by shots inside the cabin and then again out front. Something must have gone wrong.

Sixteen deaders had already entered the cabin and another eleven had staggered around back where more shooting had taken place. The Beta groaned, catching the attention of the remaining eight. It groaned again, pointing to the front of the cabin.

The pack staggered around the front, with the State

Trooper Beta leading them.

CHRIS ROUNDED THE corner of the cabin and ran into a
deader in a pair of Levi's and a tattered Patriots sweatshirt. It
snarled. Chris retreated several paces and fired a three-round
burst into its face, shattering its head. The deader dropped, its
neck oozing congealed blood into the dirt. Two more approached. Chris aimed and fired three rounds at the closest,
ripping its head apart. The second, a female in a leather biker's
outfit, drew closer. He fired two more rounds, shocked when
the deader ducked out of the way at the last moment. It
continued toward him. Having expended his ammunition,
Chris fell back again and switched out magazines.

Shithead's barking caught his attention. Off to his right,
nine more deaders came around the other side of the cabin and
lumbered toward him. He would need more fire power if he
hoped to survive.

Running back to the Humvee, Chris crawled inside, locking
the door behind him, and climbed through the mount.
Swinging the machine gun toward the pack of nine deaders, he
squeezed the trigger. Nothing happened.

Shit, he had used up the case of .50 caliber rounds.

KIERA FIRED AT each deader as they entered the bedroom,
taking out seven of them before she ran out of ammunition.

Diana had already climbed onto the roof and waited to
help Brian. The young man stepped aside.

"You go first," he told Kiera. "It'll take me a minute."

Kiera crawled onto the roof and moved aside, loading her
last round into the Mossberg.

Diana waved to Brian. "Hurry."

Brian climbed through, finding it difficult to maneuver
because of the cast. He slipped and started sliding down the

roof, catching his fall at the last moment by grabbing the sill with his good hand.

A deader, an older woman in a blood-soaked nightgown, reached the window and bit into his knuckles.

"No!" Diana punched it in the face repeatedly. On the fifth blow, the elderly female deader released her grip and snarled at Diana.

Brian pulled his hand away and slid down the slanted roof. Diana reached out for him and missed. He dropped off the end. A moment later, they heard a thud as he hit the ground, followed by snarls and his screams of terror as deaders tore him apart.

"Brian!" Anguish filled Diana's voice.

The elderly female deader reached through the window, grabbed Diana by the hair, and pulled her back. Its teeth sank into her neck. Diana thrashed about, trying to break free, but its grip was too tight. A second deader reached through, clasped Diana under her left shoulder, and pulled her back into the house. Three others converged around her, each taking a bite out of the woman's face and neck. Diana kicked her legs violently in a futile attempt to escape.

Kiera raised the shotgun and fired her last round into Diana's chest, putting her out of her misery and ensuring the poor woman would not reanimate.

With no further resistance from their meal, the deaders dragged Diana's body into the center of the room and consumed it.

NATHAN LED THE way through the woods. Rebecca brought up the rear, looking over her shoulder every few seconds for any deaders in pursuit. None had caught up with them yet.

Alissa kept pace with Steve and Miriam, the former limping because of his wounded leg, the latter walking with a grimace of pain and her hips arched forward.

She moved closer to Miriam. "Are you okay?"

"I hurt my back when I fell off the deck. It didn't help that the deader fell on top of me."

"Any internal pain?"

"No. At least, not yet. My back will be sore in the morning."

"If we make it to morning," added Steve.

"Don't worry." Nathan glanced over his shoulder. "We'll make it."

"Where are we heading?" asked Alissa.

"When Chris and I set up the perimeter fence, we ran out of barbed wire and had to leave a portion incomplete. There is more than enough room for us to crawl under it. We'll be fine once we make it to that point."

THE NATIONAL GUARD Beta hovered in the woods thirty feet from the barbed wire fence. It stood out of sight, using a tree as cover, while ten members of the pack gathered behind nearby bushes. As instructed by Alpha, it and the sheriff's deputy Beta had circled around the compound, leaving a deader behind at intervals to warn the others if prey approached. Most of the fence had been well constructed, making it difficult for any living thing to pass through. Yet at this location, the fence had not been completed, leaving a gap along the ground that would be easy to pass through. A gut feeling told it the humans would try to escape at this point.

If they did, National Guard Beta had an ambush waiting for them.

THE STATE TROOPER Beta watched Chris enter the Humvee and climb through the mount to the machine gun. It recalled a similar vehicle and weapon wreaking havoc on the pack a long time ago. A frontal assault on the human would be deadly. It quickly adapted its plan.

It moaned, attracting the attention of its pack, and pointed to the front of the Humvee. The deaders surged forward, surrounding the hood. The State Trooper Beta circled around, planning to attack the human from the rear.

The female biker Beta noticed what the other Beta had planned and headed for the rear of the Humvee, allowing its single deader to join the others in the frontal assault.

KIERA SAT TO the right of the window, her back against the cabin and holding the Mossberg. On the other side of the roof, Connie sobbed, devastated by watching her brother and mother being devoured by deaders. Little Stevie leaned across the carrier, trying to comfort her.

A deader in a FedEx uniform stuck its head out the window and, upon seeing the children, snarled. Kiera repeatedly slammed the stock of her Mossberg against its head until the skull caved in. Brains and chunks of skull dripped onto the roof. The body fell back inside the bedroom.

Kiera executed the same move on the next few deaders that stuck their heads through the window. A male teenage deader with half its shirt torn off peered out. Upon spotting Kiera, it snarled and reached for her. Kiera moved away from the window. Stepping on the pile of corpses inside the bedroom, it hoisted itself over the sill and crawled out.

CHRIS GRABBED A full case of ammunition and switched it out with the empty one. Eight deaders gathered around the front of the Humvee, scratching at the hood. They were too close for him to lower the machine gun. No matter. Reaching back inside, he picked up his AK-47 and took them down one by one with single shots to their heads.

Focusing on the immediate threat and with all the noise

from the battle, he did not notice the two Betas crawling onto the hatch and climbing up the Humvee behind him.

"THERE IT IS." Nathan ran ahead to the fence and scanned the area on the other side for danger. He saw none. Dropping to the ground, he scurried through the gap in the barbed wire and stood when on the other side, providing cover for the others.

Alissa went through next, helping Miriam and Steve who found it more difficult to negotiate the gap due to their injuries. Once they were through, Rebecca joined them.

THE NATIONAL GUARD Beta waited until all five humans were through then groaned. As one, the pack emerged from behind the bushes and attacked.

The Beta raised its head like a wolf and issued a loud, pro-longed moan, telling the others prey had been located. The sheriff deputy Beta and every deader along the line broke ranks and stumbled toward the call, converging on the humans.

Chapter Twenty-Three

"**F**UCK!" ALISSA RAISED her Mossberg and fired. Caught by surprise, her aim was off. The rounds torn into the hunter deader's chest, peppering it with buckshot and blasting a hole out its back that covered those to its rear with gore. The deader staggered back for a moment and resumed its assault.

Nathan stepped in front of her.

"Reload while I take care of this."

As Alissa loaded more shells, Nathan aimed the FAL at the hunter deader and fired at its jaw. The round punched through its open mouth and obliterated the limbic system. It dropped to the dirt with a sickening thud.

Rebecca moved to the other side of Alissa. The two performed single-round headshots on each deader, waiting until one had dropped before switching targets. By the time the pack had been eliminated, other deaders from along the perimeter stumbled into the area.

"Should we make a run for it?" asked Miriam.

Alissa shook her head. "We don't know how many more are out here. Our best bet is to get on the other side of the fence where we can take them down without getting eaten."

"Just to let you know," said Steve, "We have company on this side of the fence as well."

The deaders from the cabin that had been chasing them had finally caught up with their pray.

"I'm out," said Nathan.

Alissa stepped forward and took out the closest deader as

Nathan reloaded.

"What about those?" asked Miriam, referring to the dead-ers closing in from the rear.

"I got this." Rebecca fell prone, rolled under the gap in the fence, and climbed to her feet. She fired at the nearest, an overweight male whose stomach strained against its shirt. The first two rounds slammed into its abdomen. It burst open, spilling decayed intestines onto the ground, the nauseating stench of decay and feces filling the air. Rebecca vomited.

Nathan slammed the new magazine into the FAL and turned to Miriam and Steve. "Both of you get on the other side of the fence while you have the chance."

Miriam slid under first followed by Steve. The latter rolled rather than crawled. Three strands of barbed wire dug into his shirt and skin.

"Damn it, I'm caught."

Miriam crouched to help her husband get free.

Deaders closed in from all sides.

THE TEENAGE DEADER had crawled halfway through the window. Kiera scooted over and kicked it in the head as hard as possible, disorienting it. She grabbed its belt and yanked, dragging it out. It slid on the congealed blood, tumbling down the roof and falling to the ground below.

Before Kiera knew what had happened, another deader, a female with its blonde hair in a disheveled ponytail, reached through the window and grabbed her by the hair.

CHRIS HAD BROUGHT down the living dead in front of the Humvee when he heard Shithead barking toward the rear of the vehicle. A snarl came from behind him. He spun his head in time to see the State Trooper Beta crawling up the hatch, only inches away.

He dropped back inside, barely missing being bitten. The deader centered itself in the hatch and climbed in after him. Chris withdrew his revolver and fired six rounds into its head. The first four tore it apart, covering Chris in fragments of skull and brains. The last two sailed harmlessly through empty air. Its dead weight dragged the female biker Beta inside the vehicle where the body fell onto Chris. Shithead had enough sense to jump in the back, avoiding getting hit by the corpse. Chris screamed, shoved the body off him, and exited the Humvee.

When he did, the female biker Beta jumped off the roof, landing on Chris' back and knocking him to the ground.

REBECCA WIPED THE vomit from her mouth with the back of her hand. A second deader lunged at her. Rebecca kicked it away. As it struggled to regain its footing, she fired three rounds into its head, dropping it. She switched fire to a third and took that one out as well.

In the meantime, Steve had panicked, digging the barbs deeper into his arm.

"Hold still," yelled Miriam.

Steve calmed down.

Miriam grabbed his arm with one hand and the strand in the other then ripped. He winced as the barbs tore three pieces of flesh from his arm. Once free, Miriam lifted the strand and Steve rolled to the relative safety of the inner compound.

The smell of blood drove the remaining deaders into a frenzy and they pressed home their attack.

The National Guard Beta emerged from behind the tree and closed in for the kill, hoping the humans' attention would be drawn to the rest of the pack.

Alissa and Nathan continued their assault. Neither wanted to abandon the other and be caught vulnerable while on the ground trying to escape. Both stood their ground and gunned down anything that got close.

ALPHA EMERGED FROM the woods to witness the last stand of the humans. It felt a sense of satisfaction. The assault on the cabin may have failed but the ambush had succeeded. The deaders it had sent around back had caught the humans trying to escape. They were surrounded. In a few minutes, the pack would feed.

Alpha approached the carnage, using the woods for cover.

KIERA JERKED HER head forward and rolled to the side, pulling the ponytail deader through the window onto the roof. It started to slide. Kiera felt a wave of terror rush through her as she thought she might be pulled off the slope with it. The deader released its grip at the last minute, using both hands to stop its sliding.

It noticed Little Stevie and Connie in the corner and climbed toward them.

Kiera scrambled over to help the kids. Another deader in a camouflage hunting jacket emerged through the window, snarling and clutching at her, and blocking her path to the children.

THE DEPUTY BETA drew nearer to the ambush. The gunfire continued, so it had not missed out on feeding.

Ahead of it, two humans were on this side of the fence fighting a last-ditch battle to prevent the inevitable. Three more were on the opposite side, their attention focused toward the cabin.

Moving into the woods so it could approach undetected, the deputy Beta moved waited for its opportunity to move in for the kill.

CHRIS COULD NOT move. The female biker Beta had him

pinned to the ground. He closed his eyes and waited for the deader to bite his neck.

A growl came from behind him and he felt the deader's body shift. Chris glanced over his shoulder. Shithead had jumped out of the Humvee and bitten down on the deader's belt, pulling it off his master. The Beta switched its attention to the animal, swiping at Shithead and trying to brush him away.

Chris backward kicked the deader twice, shoving it off him. Once free, he got to his feet and spun around.

"Hey, asshole."

The female biker Beta made eye contact with him.

Chris kicked it twice in the face, knocking out several teeth and dislocating its lower jaw. It issued a gurgling snarl and tried to stand, but the weight of the dog prevented that. Chris kicked it two more times in the face, cracking its skull and dislodging an eye from its socket. The Beta's head fell to the dirt.

Chris stomped on its head. On the third strike, its skull fractured into several pieces. He stomped again. The female biker Beta's head erupted like a rotten melon, its brains bursting through the skin. Chris stomped on the brain several times until the deader stopped moving.

Shaken by the near-death experience, Chris fell against the front fender of the Humvee and slid down the side. Shithead raised a leg, pissed on the remains of the Beta's head, then ran over to his master and licked his face.

"You're a good boy." Chris hugged the dog. Shithead's tail wagged.

Gunfire came from behind the cabin. This fight was far from over.

Standing up, Chris dragged the corpse from the Humvee, retrieved his AK-47 and bag of ammunition, and shut the door.

"Come on boy. We have to help the others."

"ALISSA," YELLED REBECCA. "To your left."

She turned into time to see the National Guard Beta approaching. With the humans concentrating on the deaders along the fence, it had moved toward the gap between them, hoping to take them by surprise. It would have worked if the female human had not issued the warning.

Alissa fired. It ducked to the left, the pellets punching into its chest and shoulder. A few caught it in the face, penetrating its right eye. Oblivious to the pain, it moved in for the kill.

Alissa pulled the trigger again, but her Mossberg had run out of ammunition. It stepped forward, clutched her by the collar, and leaned its head forward to bite.

Seeing what was about to happen, Nathan shoved the barrel of the FAL into its mouth. It glared at him, realizing it had miscalculated. Nathan fired. Its head exploded, covering Alissa's face and chest in gore. Nathan withdrew the weapon and the National Guard Beta's lifeless body fell into the dirt.

CONNIE SCREAMED AND cried as the ponytail deader approached but she refused to go down without a fight. She waited until it had crawled to within two feet of her. Raising her leg, she kicked it in the face. Once. Twice. Three times. The deader released its grip on the roof to grab her leg. Connie kicked it in the jaw, sending the ponytail deader sliding down the roof and over the edge. Still screaming, Connie held the carrier for dear life. Little Stevie reached out with his left arm and wrapped it around her shoulder.

The hunter deader in the window managed to grab Kiera's arm and drew her close. She had only one option left. Kiera stuck her thumbs into the deader's eyes and shoved them back as far as they would go. It howled and released its grip. Kiera scooted to the opposite corner of the roof, wiped her thumbs on her pants legs, and vomited in her lap.

The hunter deader remained in the window, flailing its arms in a desperate attempt to find its prey, and blocking the others from getting to the roof.

CHRIS AND SHITHEAD ran around to the left side of the house and into six deaders. One lay on the ground, its head at almost a ninety-degree angle to its neck. He assumed it had somehow broken its neck since the body did not move but the head snarled and snapped at him. Another crawled along the dirt, its legs broken. Four others stood by the wall, clawing as if they wanted to climb it.

Shithead barked.

"Shit."

One of the deaders clawing at the wall was Brian. His abdomen and left arm had been devoured, exposing his internal organs and spine. The four stumbled toward him.

Chris raised the AK-47 and took down each with a shot to the head. Withdrawing his revolver, he stepped over, double tapped the two immobile deaders, then double tapped Brian.

"Who's there?"

"Kiera, is that you?"

"Uncle Chris, I'm so glad to see you."

"Where are you?"

"Up here. On the roof."

Chris moved away from the house and saw Kiera, Little Stevie, and Connie pressed against the wall of the cabin.

Kiera waved. "We're trapped by a bunch of deaders inside. Can you help us?"

"I'll be right there."

Chris and Shithead circled around front and went back inside the cabin.

ALISSA AND NATHAN took out the last of the deaders along the fence line. Neither had much ammunition left. Another few minutes and they would have been overrun.

She listened. There were no more moans, only the furious chirping of birds agitated by all the noise.

Alissa heard gunfire coming from the cabin. "We need to check on the others.

Nathan crouched down and started to pass through the gap in the fence. As he did, Alpha emerged from the woods and charged, clutching Alissa's shoulder from behind.

ENTERING THE CABIN, Chris found seven deaders wandering aimlessly on the first level. He took them out quickly. Switching out his magazine with a full one, he and Shithead made their way through the mass of corpses, watching each carefully so as not to be attacked, and headed up to the bedrooms, carefully negotiating their way around the dead bodies on the stairs and landing.

Chris heard a pack of deaders in Alissa's bedroom. Rushing down the hall, he peered through the doorway. Diana's half-devoured corpse lay in the center of the floor. Deaders were crumbled in front of the window with another tried to crawl over them. Four stood around it, scratching at the windows, trying to get to the kids outside. Aiming low so that stray rounds would not punch through the walls, he fired a sustained burst, blasting away their legs. The deaders collapsed to the floor. Moving over to the window, he finished them off with a bullet to each head. Shouldering his AK-47, Chris grabbed the deader in the window by the legs and pulled it back inside. It fell face first on the floor. Unholstering his revolver, he fired two rounds into its skull.

An eerie silence fell over the bedroom.

"It's clear."

Kiera centered herself in the window. Upon seeing Chris, she climbed through, nearly slipping on the pile of corpses, and raced over to him. She embraced him around the waist and lay her head against his chest.

"Thank God you showed up," she cried. "I thought we were goners."

"It's okay. You're safe now." Chris patted Kiera on the back of her head. "Let's get the others."

Connie came through first.

"Did you see my brother down there?"

"Yes."

"He's dead?"

"I'm sorry."

Connie sobbed. Kiera pulled the girl close to her.

Little Stevie pushed the carrier in front of the window. Chris brought it inside and then helped the boy into the bedroom. The kid thanked him with a high-five.

"Where did the others go?" asked Chris.

"The escaped out back." Kiera became concerned. "Do you think they're okay?"

Chris listened. No more gunfire came from the woods.

"I'm sure they'll be back soon." Chris hoped he was not telling the kids a lie.

FROM ITS HIDING place, the sheriff's deputy Beta watched Alpha attack the female human on this side of the fence. It left the safety of the woods to help its leader.

ALISSA DROPPED THE Mossberg and slammed her head backwards, her skull catching Alpha in the face and preventing it from biting her. The blow broke its nose and loosened two teeth, the deader unmindful of the pain. She continued the pummeling, praying she wouldn't accidentally cut herself on its teeth.

Nathan crawled backed under the fence. He moved around to Alpha's rear and yanked the deader off Alissa. It turned and went after him. Nathan drove the palm of his hand into its face, hoping to disorient it. Rather than stagger away, as Nathan had predicted, Alpha knocked the human's arm out of the way and lunged, knocking Nathan over. He fell back onto the grass with enough force that it momentarily knocked the wind out of him. Alpha bent over to bite Nathan, taking him out of the battle.

Before Alpha could do so, Alissa wrapped her left arm around Alpha's neck, the inside of her elbow against its Adam's apple, the upper and lower arms tightening on its arteries. It thrashed around, trying to shake her off. Alissa had used the tactic out of instinct, forgetting that such a move would not render the living dead unconscious. Alissa realized that if she let go now, the deader would more than likely kill her.

The sheriff's deputy Beta, seeing its opportunity with both humans distracted, rushed forward.

Rebecca stood on the other side of the fence, her weapon raised, waiting for the chance to fire on the deader attacking Alissa and Nathan without risking killing her friends. She spotted movement out of the corner of her eye and saw a second deader rushing toward Nathan, who remained stunned. Spinning the weapon in its direction, she fired. The first round missed. The second two tore into its chest, ripping out chunks of flesh and shredding organs. The sheriff's deputy Beta faltered but continued, determined to feed. Rebecca steadied her aim and pulled the trigger. The weapon clicked. She had used the last of her ammunition.

The gunfire had snapped Nathan back to reality. The Beta was only a few yards away about to pounce. Sliding his Sig Sauer out of its holster, he had time for only one shot. Nathan pulled the trigger. The round caught the deader underneath the jaw, ripping its way up and through its head, destroying the limbic system in the process. The sheriff's deputy Beta collapsed, falling onto the ground beside Nathan.

Miriam crawled under the fence and picked up Alissa's Mossberg. Circling around to in front of her friend, she rammed the stock into the deader's face, careful not to slip and hit Alissa instead.

"Don't worry about me," said Alissa. "Bash it harder."

Alissa lowered her head as Miriam rammed the Mossberg into Alpha's face again, knocking out several teeth.

A long-forgotten emotion filled Alpha – fear. This should not be happening. It was the leader. Its pack had overpowered every human they had encountered. The concept of defeat had never entered its primitive mind. Yet it knew, like a cornered animal about to die, that its only chance of survival was to fight back ferociously. When the weapon smashed into its face for the third time, Alpha growled and attacked Miriam, dragging Alissa with it.

Alissa tried to hold it back and stumbled in the process. When she glanced down to regain her footing, she saw her hunting knife strapped to her leg. She had forgotten about it in the middle of the carnage. Sliding it from its sheath, she stepped to the side, exposing the deader's neck, and plunged the blade into the gap where the spine connects with the skull.

For Alpha, everything went blank when the knife penetrated its brain. The insatiable hunger. The skills of the hunt. The current battle. Only a brief image flashed through its mind of a female and a male child, humans that had once been dear to it and brought it comfort. The memory ended when Alissa twisted the knife, churning the blade through its limbic system and ending its existence. When she withdrew the knife, Alpha's body slid to the dirt in front of her.

Alissa and the others scanned the area around them, searching for more deaders. They did not see or hear anything for several seconds.

"Is it really over?" asked Miriam.

"I think so." Alissa drew in a deep breath. "We made it."

"Thank God," said Rebecca.

"Not everyone did." Nathan stood and extended his right hand, the palm up, exposing teeth marks above the wrist. "I was bit when I struck the deader in the face."

"No!" Alissa raced over to Nathan and examined his hand. Its teeth had penetrated the skin and bit deep into the tissue. This wasn't a scratch with a chance he might survive. This wound was a death sentence.

"No." This time Alissa sobbed the word and pulled Nathan close to her, holding him tight.

Chapter Twenty-Four

CHRIS PACED BACK and forth outside the cabin, watching for any surviving deaders while waiting for the others to return. Only ten minutes had elapsed, but it seemed like hours. Shithead stayed with him, alert to the tension and eyeing his master every few seconds. The kids were inside. After checking the cabin for deaders, which there were none still alive, Chris had told them to stay in their parents' room until he came for them.

Shithead growled. A moment later, Chris heard something approaching through the trees. He readied to open fire, thankful to see Alissa and the others emerge from the tree line. His hopes collapsed when he saw the despair on her face. He asked one simple question.

"Who?"

Nathan forced a smile and showed him the bite on his hand. "Me."

"Shit," Chris mumbled.

"Excuse me." Alissa took Nathan's good hand. "I have to get him inside and tend to the wound."

"You know that's not going to work," said Nathan.

"I can at least try," she snapped and led him toward the cabin.

Miriam ran up to Chris and took his hands. Her voice quivered. "Kiera and Stevie... are they...?"

"They're fine. Both are waiting in your room with Connie and Archer."

"What about Diana and Brian?" asked Steve.

"They didn't make it."

"Dear God." Miriam bowed her head and uttered a silent prayer. "We should get inside."

"Let me warn you, it's a slaughterhouse in there."

"I don't care. I need to see my kids."

The kids heard their parents and met them at the door. Miriam dropped to her knees and held them tight. Connie stayed in the background, grieving over the loss of her own family. Miriam released her children and waved the young girl over. Connie rushed into her arms and sobbed on Miriam's shoulder. The rest of the family closed in and joined in a group hug for their new member.

Chris moved away from the reunion and headed upstairs to Rebecca's room, which had been unscathed in the carnage. Nathan lay on the bed and Alissa examined the wound. She rose from the bed and headed for the door.

"Stay with him. I'll get the first aid kit."

Nathan clasped her hand. "That won't do any good."

"You don't know that." Alissa broke his grip and raced out of the room.

Chris strolled over to the bed. "I'm sorry."

"It's not your fault. It was bound to happen to one of us eventually. I'm glad it didn't happen to Alissa or one of the kids."

"Yeah." Chris struggled for the right words. "So, how do you want to do this?"

"What do you mean?"

"Do you want one of us to take you out or do you prefer to do it yourself?"

"I can't take my own life. I don't want to go to Hell."

"Under the circumstances. I think God will forgive you."

"I'd rather not take any chances." Nathan forced a chuckle. "Tie my hands to the bed and, when the time comes, I want you to kill me. Please don't make Alissa do it. I don't want her to have to make that decision."

"You have my promise, buddy." Chris stepped forward and the two men shook hands. Chris patted Nathan's hand and squeezed.

Alissa came back into the room with a first aid kit and sat on the bed beside Nathan. She went through the motions of cleaning and bandaging Nathan's wound, clearly trying to avoid the inevitable.

PREVIEW OF *NURSE ALISSA VS. THE ZOMBIES V: DESPERATE MISSION*

3 March

This cabin will never be the same again – and I'm not talking just physically.

    The deader attack yesterday tore this place apart. Both the front and kitchen doors were ripped out of their jambs by the horde. Chris and Steve remounted them last night, but it was a jury-rigged effort. The hinges are fragile. The doors don't open and close properly and are unable to withstand anything pushing on them. The windows in front were shot out by machine gun fire and the twin glass doors leading out to the deck were shattered by the deaders. Thankfully, Paul had stored pre-cut plywood in the shed to cover them. Chris and Steve are planning on a run to a hardware store in the next few days to pick up replacement for the ones that are broken. Even so, nothing will repair all the bullet holes, hundreds of them. Most of them are along the porch where Chris gunned down the horde trying to get inside with the .50 caliber. There are quite a few on the interior walls from the battle inside the cabin. Those will also serve as a constant reminder of just how unsafe this world is.

    Plus, there are hundreds of corpses inside and outside the cabin, all but two of them deaders. Chris and Steve dug two graves near the tree line for Diana and Brian and gave them a proper burial last night. They wanted to dig a third one for Nathan but I refused. Nathan will be gone soon enough. Digging his grave beforehand seems morbid. They're working now on removing and disposing of the deaders, and then will help Miriam and Rebecca clean and disinfect the place. Even so, none of us will ever erase the images of the carnage that took place here and the gory aftermath.

My room is a battle zone. Chris won't let me go in there until they're restored it to order, which I don't mind. I've been sitting in Nathan's room all night with him, a Colt in my lap. Ready to put him out of his misery once he turns.

The cabin has lost all meaning to me. I used to view it as a safe haven, the place I had escaped to in order to avoid the nightmare enveloping the rest of the world. How fucking naïve. Now it's just a location to hide out in, a place to stay until we're killed or forced to run. Chris has been trying to reassure me that everything will be fine, that this was a fluke that will never be repeated. I'm not sure if he believes that. I don't. Our sanctuary was violated once and I'm stuck with the realization that it could, and probably will, happen again.

The violation of our sanctuary was also a violation of my sense of security. I no longer feel confident that we'll survive this apocalypse.

The worst part is sitting here waiting to mercy Nathan, my best friend and my lover, the man who saved my life on more than one occasion. I'm no stranger to death, even before this whole nightmare began. I've watched many patients die in the ER. I even watched my mother pass away from cancer and my father die of loneliness several months later. This is different. I never had an emotional bond with my patients and was helpless to do anything to help my parents. Sure, I helped that old man in the hospital die, left many others to their fate, and killed people when that gang attacked us. That was different. This is the first time that I'll be taking the life of someone I care for. It hurts. The idea leaves me cold and dead inside.

I hate to say this, but I wish Nathan would hurry up and turn so I can end his suffering and get this over with.

"GRAB HIS ARMS," Chris ordered Steve.

The two men lifted the deader off the kitchen floor and carried it through the living area and off to the side where they piled it on top of the funeral pyre Chris had set up last night. He had found in the storage shed several pallets that Paul had loaded supplies on, placed them on the ground, and doused them with kerosene. The two men had stacked the corpses on top of the pallets ten layers deep, each layer doused with more kerosene and with firewood laid between them. They would light it later tonight when the dark would conceal the smoke from anyone, or anything, nearby. He had picked the side of the compound to protect the cabin and hopefully keep the flames from being seen along the road.

"That takes care of those inside and some from the porch." Steve paused to catch his breath. "What about the hundreds outside?"

"We'll worry about those later."

"Are you planning on burning those as well?"

"I doubt we have enough gasoline and wood to take care of them all. Those in the woods we'll leave for now. The rest we'll drag over here to get them away from the cabin." Chris swatted away the bloated flied and wasps that hovered over the dead and strayed toward him. "We're going to have to find a pick-up truck and haul them away. Once that's done, we can get what we need to repair the cabin."

"A lot easier said than done."

"Yeah." Chris stared at the cabin where Alissa kept a death watch over Nathan. "But I'd rather do this than what Alissa has to go through."

A GENTLE KNOCK sounded on the bedroom door. Alissa snapped awake, realizing she had dozed off. The notebook and pen fell out of her lap. She grabbed the Colt, ready to shoot Nathan, but he lay in bed, still asleep.

The knock came again and Miriam asked, "Can I come in?"

"Sure."

Miriam entered holding a cup of coffee and a plate with a sandwich. "I thought you might want these. You skipped breakfast this morning."

"Thanks." Alissa did not feel like eating, but coffee sure sounded good.

Miriam placed the cup and plate on the dresser. Alissa picked up the cup and took a long sip. "Thanks. I needed that. I started dozing off."

"You need to get your sleep."

"I will when…" Alissa let her words trail off.

"How's Nathan doing?"

Alissa glanced over at the bed. Nathan lay in a restless slumber. His hands and feet had been tied to the bed frame so he couldn't move. His breathing was steady though a bit belabored. Half an hour ago, he had been tossing his head and mumbling, but had quieted down after a few minutes.

"He's not doing well. His wound is becoming infected and he's running a fever of one hundred and two degrees. I've given him anti-biotics, but those will take a few days to work."

"I'm surprised he hasn't turned yet." Miriam regretted her words. "Sorry. I didn't mean to sound so callous."

"It's okay. I am, too." According to everything she had witnessed in Boston, those infected reanimated quickly. By all accounts, Nathan should have turned within an hour of being bitten by the deader, at most. Instead, he lingered in this damnable limbo.

"Do you think he's immune?"

"No, unfortunately," Alissa remembered Dr. Edwards from

Mass General on the first day of the outbreak. He had been bitten but didn't turn. Dr. Edwards had showed no symptoms of infection and bled out rather than succumb to the virus. If Nathan was immune, he should be conscious.

"I wish there was something we could do for Nathan."

"Maybe there is." Alissa felt a glimmer of hope well up inside of her. "Where's Steve?"

"Helping Chris remove the bodies from the cabin."

"Here." Alissa stood and handed Miriam the Colt. "Stay here and let me know if Nathan… if there's any change in his condition."

Alissa ran out of the bedroom and headed downstairs.

A Thank You to My Readers

I like to think of myself as a storyteller. I've been writing short stories as far back as I can remember, but it was Darren McGavin as *The Night Stalker*'s Carl Kolchak that inspired me to be become a full-time writer. Writing and working for the CIA have been two of the most fulfilling things I've done with my life. The best part is having people who read my books, enjoy them, and want more. I'm extremely fortunate and grateful that I have a fanbase that devours my novels like zombies eating human flesh. You keep reading and I'll keep writing.

If you liked *Nurse Alissa vs. the Zombies IV: Hunters*, please post a review on Amazon and/or Goodreads. It doesn't have to be long—just a rating and a sentence or two about why you enjoyed it. The more reviews the *Nurse Alissa vs. the Zombies* series receives, the more opportunity other readers have of discovering the book.

The *Nurse Alissa* saga will continue. Books five and six are being written and plotted now. Alissa and her group will be teaming up with the military for a bit, which means plenty of deader action and some highly unique ways to kill off the living dead. After that, the (few?) survivors might go on a road trip. New Mexico sounds fun.

A second series, which is post-apocalyptic but without zombies, is in pre-production (i.e. I'm researching and plotting out the concept). Expect the first book in that series sometime in early 2021 – that is, if we make it through 2020.

Acknowledgments

Writing is solitary and lonely. Getting a book published, on the other hand, is a complicated process involving many people, all of whom deserve to be recognized.

A major thanks goes out to my beta readers who have been with me from book one: Tammy Michelle Mayberry, Michael Atkinson, Pammy Troupe, Tom Williamson, Marla Dewitt, Dan Uebel, Norma Seitz, Roseann Powell, Doc Fried, Paul Semke, and Cari Laffrenier Thompson. They point out grammatical/spelling errors, plot flaws, inconsistencies (like the time I killed a character, brought him back to life a few chapters later, and then killed him again), and offer their opinion on whether they like the story. I would be lost without them.

Christian Bentulan designed the cover art for *Nurse Alissa vs. the Zombies IV: Hunters* as well as the other books in the saga. I love Christian's work. His covers reach out and grab the reader's attention as well as foreshadow what is to come. Plus, Archer appears on each cover, which he appreciates.

You would not be reading this book, or any of the other in the *Nurse Alissa* series, were it not for my dear friend and colleague Alina Giuchici. I hadn't written a zombie series since *Rotter Apocalypse* was published in 2015. Alina is a major fan of my stories and kept urging me to go back to writing about the living dead. With some gentle shoving in the right direction and a few well-placed ideas, over the course of a long week on the road I came up with the concept of the Alissa series. If you like these books, be sure to thank Alina.

Finally, a major debt of thanks goes to my family, human and furry. The past few months have been difficult between the new job that requires me to be at work by 0400, severe family illnesses, and trying to juggle everything myself. It's hard to maintain my writing discipline right now, but I couldn't do this without their love and support.

About the Author

Scott M. Baker was born and raised in Everett, Massachusetts and spent twenty-three years in northern Virginia working for the Central Intelligence Agency. Scott is now retired and lives just outside of Concord, New Hampshire with his wife and fellow writer Alison Beightol, stepdaughter, two rambunctious boxers, and two cats who treat him as their human servant. He is currently writing the *Nurse Alissa vs. the Zombies* saga, his latest zombie apocalypse series, and the *Shattered World* series, his five-book young adult post-apocalypse thriller about a group of adventurers attempting to close interdimensional portals into Hell. Previous works include *The Vampire Hunters* trilogy, about humans fighting the undead in Washington D.C.; *Rotter World, Rotter Nation*, and *Rotter Apocalypse*, his first post-apocalyptic zombie saga; *Yeitso*, his homage to the giant monster movies of the 1950s that he loved watching as a kid; as well as several zombie-themed novellas and anthologies.

Please check out Scott's social media accounts for the latest information on future books, upcoming events, and other fun stuff.

Blog: scottmbakerauthor.blogspot.com
Facebook: facebook.com/groups/397749347486177
Twitter: twitter.com/vampire_hunters
Instagram: instagram.com/scottmbakerwriter

www.ingramcontent.com/pod-product-compliance
Lightning Source LLC
Chambersburg PA
CBHW071924220626
47052CB00002B/451